Lady In Red

Kate Colton

Contents

‖ CHAPTER 1 ‖

Like a passing autumn leaf, I was brought from my home to a new world. Where the people couldn't be trusted, the folk tales different, their traditions different. The only question I held to myself as I sat before my mirror, was will I wilt and turn into nothing as I stepped into his world, or will I be taken by someone, cherished and loved like the last leaf of autumn.

~

"Death awaits her"

Whispered one of them who stood between the hurdle of women. The gossiping mannequins with their frilly bottoms, married and nothing to accomplish in their lives. "My sympathy with that child. How could her father do such a thing"

Spoke another prude woman with her hand over her lips as if to silence her voice but that won't do any good. Their voices are louder than glass breaking against this marble floor.

"Miss Ruby Williams"

I turned my attention from the chattering old woman to the knight who had supposedly walked up to me while I was distracted by the thoughts of others. He bowed slightly and looked down at me while his hand was directed toward the doors leading to the library. I picked up my grown and walked toward the double doors with an anxious heart. It felt as if my chest would burn through my ribcage any minute. My hands were sweaty and trembling. No matter how hot the humungous gown made me, my neck had chills.

The guards opened the double doors and I heard the ballroom go into silence before slight gossip of men and women began again. Possibly about what I was going to face as the daughter of a man who sold me off as bait to pacify the kingdom's quarrel. That man, my father, The Duke with his head hung low looked up as the King with all his glory stood ahead facing out the arch-stained glasses and his hand behind him.

"Do you know why you are summoned here, Ruby? My dear niece"

"Apart from the sympathizing gossip, I heard on my way here My king, No. I do not" I chose to stay illiterate about the real agreement. I wanted him to have the courage to say it himself. "Well, I shall be blunt then-" The king said, his hand now twisting the globe on his desk beside him to fidget as he paused to push the words out his mouth.

As I await the dreading news, I held my breath. My corset was getting tighter each second as my ability to hold my tears back and breath ceased to continue.

"I promised to grant Prince Edward your hand in marriage a month ago, I was told you two got very close through this arrangement and possibly lo-like each other -"

That was the pause I hate the most. I felt like I would fall to my knees any minute.

"But, It seems that some arrangements cannot do. Your father had no choice but to make new arrangements. That is, break your engagement with Edward and have you marry someone else" I broke into tears, my lips sealed shut as I could not speak against the King's words. His eyes finally looked at me. His brows creased as his lips opened to speak but I could see that look of worry in his eyes.

As my eyes rolled out those never-ending tears in vain because there was nothing anyone could do for me I took in deep breaths as the King spoke again.

"My power will have your back as you wed the- creature of a man. Do not fret. You will have my guards to protect you. I will make sure you will be treated as a queen should be."

My head shook from side to side slowly in disappointment. There is no power of guards when they enter the fort of another kingdom. There are only pawns in the games.

"You cannot even name the man she will marry"

A voice from behind me spoke. I heard the heels of her shoe click as she walked past me. Her long black hair sent a slight smell of orange across my face. Her golden robes dragged across the floor as her crown reflected the fire burning in that dark library.

" Lycan, Xerxes Lycan. The king who burned down a city and cursed whoever may walk upon it, kills innocent humans, salves animals, and is the ruler of all wolves who walk upon this land. She is to marry the son of Chaos itself."

I stood there as the queen spoke for me. The only human alive who could. I stood there, with my heart twisting second by second as the Queen and The King argued while my father watched this unfold.

"You are sending your niece into a land of pure evil"

"The pact is already made your highness, The treaty signed, There is nothing to be done! If we break this marriage all hell will break loose"

The queen turned to my father. Her eyes sent a duke towering over her state to his knees. "Do you realize how much of a shame you are to society, Sir Aiden Williams?"

I saw my father gulp. The king closed his eyes in defeat and gave a sigh.

"I have to come to that child's aid while her own father sold her to a man who isn't even human. I had taken great pleasure raising your daughter under my wing as one of my ladies in waiting Sir. Giving her all that was required to be a princess on a day when she marries the right man. Prince ·Edward! It seems so, that all my teachings were in vain!"

I couldn't hold back as my throat choked. A soft cry filled the echoing walls of the library as they turned their heads to me. I stood there helpless, while my tears ran down my chin and my mouth trembled while I suffocated in that dark place.

The Queen was not the type of woman to feel emotions. It was a belief that after the loss of her third child, she became a ruthless ruler. And she could bend any and everyone under her feet but that dark King. He could never be bent. He was a werewolf, an enemy.

I never cared for who they were. I saw them as creatures made by god-like we were. They were respected and were much more powerful. I never saw them as an enemy personally, I only saw them as humans with a different life.

But breaking my marriage with the man I loved, sending me into the hands of a man who enslaves thousand. Where I would have no protection of my title nor my kingdom was so cruel. My father had betrayed me. The Queen looked at me with eyes of sorrow, which was something she never did.

"You are a disappointment to your daughter," She said her last words to him as she stormed out of the library. She stopped as the doors opened.

"Ruby, I expect you to be in my privy chambers tomorrow"

I didn't even nod as I ought to. I just glanced at my father once before turning around and walking out the doors. I went straight down the halls to the back of the castle and out the gardens.

I couldn't even see him for the last time as I would just break. I imagined my life with Edward, and now it was destroyed.

***

She twisted and turned in her bed all night as the new moon darken the sky, the clouds were heading toward the castle as mist covered the grasslands. Winter was near and the leaves shed as a chilly breeze ran across the grounds. It was a beautiful night indeed however for Ruby, it was a night she would never forget filled with dread. And soon her eyes closed as she could no more shed tears and think.

That morning she walked through the walls of the castle towards the Queen's chambers reporting to her duty as everyone man, guard, maiden and worker stepped aside and bowed, some only watched as Ruby walked past them. She noticed their behaviour, but she chose to let it pass like the wind.

From the first day after the announcement of the Kingdom's treaty with King Xerxes, Ruby became a Queen to another throne. As she walked the halls of the court, all those who stood ahead stepped aside and bowed as they ought to. She was no longer just a woman born in the royals. She was no longer a young maiden serving under the Queen. The high respect she was held under in the last few days of her life in her birthday kingdom had only been seen as a sacrifice.

"Your Highness"

Ruby gave her greetings with courtesy as the Queen turned around and stood up from her vanity. Ruby walked towards her curtains to tie them back but her hands were stopped. She never looked up to the Queen.

"I am truly sorry for what has happened."

Ruby shook her head softly with a smile of sorrow and pulled her hand back. "It is my duty now."

Queen glanced at the other maidens and the room was left of just them two. And the doors shut close the Queen walked towards her desk and sat on her chair.

"And it is my duty as the Queen to tell you about what will be expected of you-"

"An heir" Ruby whispered, with her back towards the crown she glanced at the Queen once before turning her head towards the windows again. She watched the cloudy sky and took a deep breath.

"If my head is hanging on a blade until I produce an heir then yes, The king will have his heir"

‖ CHAPTER 2 ‖

I was adorned with jewels, pinning some of my strands behind my hair, and was let down with a bow and pearls embedded on the back. I watched as the maids fussed around me while I stood there embarrassed, in my innerwear. I gulp letting one of the maids put my corset on, I suck in my breath as she pulled and laced me up, my hands staying on my stomach while the other is on the desk ahead. I stare at the jewels on my neck and my ears.

I was being bejeweled for what? I was already given up to the man who will be taking me back to his castle. There was no need for flattery. I blinked several times in frustration.

"Madam" Bowed one maid behind me and I turned to see the gown. My eyes stare at the dark red gown she placed delicately on the chair.

As I stared at that blood-red fabric the maids seemed suddenly to disappear around me. The room felt darker as I realized what the color signified. It was a disgusting thought, meaningful but disgusting. I had no hate for that man who will take me away today. But I will always despise my father for breaking my marriage and selling me off to someone else.

I blink several times to rid myself of my tears and looked around at the room surrounded by maids. I felt suffocated. My heartbeat was uneven and my hands started feeling sweaty. My legs hurt even before I stepped out the doors. My neck felt itchy and it hurt to have those jewels around me. It seemed to worsen the feeling of a chokehold on me.

My throat inside felt dry and it hurt. The feelings of holding your tears back and feeling a great amount of frustration build up in your gut and throat. As they fussed around me with my hair and touched my inner getting ready to put on that gown and suddenly blurt out, "Stop !" I paused taking a deep breath and looking at one of them.

"Get me a glass of wine please."

As stunning as a deer but calmly one of them nodded and left.

I remember my authority. However displeasing it was I spoke for the first time in those 5 hours of my grooming, "Take these off. I need to breathe not suffocate to death here." I said taking off one of the jewels and placing it over the vanity.

"But madam-"

I smile turning to her. "It is my ball, I will do as I please and dress as I please"

Do as I please for the last time that is ...

Taking off the jewels from my ears, neck, and my hands. I ask her to lace up the red gown. My neck felt much better with nothing on it. I closed my eyes as she tightened the laces while my wine glass arrive. I grab it and drown the glass down. That sour liquid was unpleasant to me. I hardly drank. I sigh keeping the glass down.

As I turned around, seeing myself in that beautiful red gown I frown. It was such a beautiful dress, The sleeves dropped down my shoulder flowing from my bust to the back of my shoulder. My cleavage was moderately visible, it sinched my waist. The skirt flowed gracefully while some of the fabric was tucked up on one side and the rest free. I felt like I was tied with ribbons, the silhouette looked perfect on me, unfortunately, I will always hate what it meant. My white hair complimented the dark shade of that dress. My complexion was fair and my cheeks were slightly tinted with rouge.

"Madam, It is time." I heard the Knight, Sir Fred.

He was introduced to me as by the governor yesterday as my personal guard under the King's orders. Fred or Fredrick as his real name was a gentleman with dark hair and a tall figure loomed over all. As we talked for the few minutes that I was introduced to him, I found him very introverted.

"Thank you for escorting me." He bowed again but all this time as his gaze stayed pinned to the ground he looked up at me for the first time and his eyes suddenly frowned in my sight. But they snapped back to the dead expression.

"What is it? Be frank with me." I asked.

"It is nothing Madam, shall we?" he asked giving me his arm to hold. But I did not move.

"Well? We are going to be companions, you might as well say it?"

He opened his mouth but closed it again and when I raised my eyebrows at him he seemed to give up the contemplation in his mind.

"I believe the maids forgot to put the given gold pearl jewels on you."

I stare at him in question.

"How do you know I was to wear them?" I ask with curiosity.

"Madam, I was the one who delivered them to your chamber under the Queen's commands." "Oh." I turn my eyes to those jewels which were now back in the boxes. "I chose to not wear them," I answer.

Sir Fred asked no more questions but nodded while encouraging me to keep my hand over his fist. I did so and we walked towards the hall door. And while I walked silently, I wondered how King Xerxes looked and acted. Would he be what they said? A cold-faced strange man who never held a conversation for more than thirty seconds. A King whose stare could kill and who with a single command would have a man's head cut off.

I felt my stomach twist and turn as the alcohol in the wine started to work in my body.As the doors opened, My eyes set on the largest golden chandelier filled with thousands of candles, and the ceiling was adorned with smaller crystal chandeliers. The walls as always grand but the golden curtains were replaced with red.

The thrones for The King and Queen were placed on the balcony right ahead. And as I lowered my eyes to the ground the ballroom was filled with people who I realized had stopped their chatter and turned to stare at me.

My heart was beating out loud as my body felt crushed under their eyes. My eyes couldn't stay on one person, they moved from side to side taking in all those who stood. I felt my hands tighten around the Knights fist.

As we slowly walked in, every step I took felt wrong.

"Before I leave you Madam, advice from your fellow lady in waiting. She advises you to avoid speaking with the men, especially the dukes and Prince Edward's family, they have been in anger since the announcement was given."

I look up at him and back at the ground. I nodded.

It was truly rude for them to hate me for what had become of this.

And through the crowd, as Sir Fred led me towards my family I saw him. Prince Edward. After a week of our last tea together when we discussed our wedding vows. I frowned and I felt sadness fill me as our eyes met. It hurt me more as we came closer to his frame and he bowed. I looked down to stop any further gossip. I was to act as if nothing have happen and it broke me from the inside.

"Ruby, My dear sweetpea."

I heard my mother's voice and I looked up. The knight bowed one last time before letting me be with my mother.

"Mumma," I whispered as she hugged me tightly.

"They wouldn't let me see you till today. They were afraid I would help you escape or feel more sorrow, I haven't spoken to your father ever since I heard about this, This is outrageous." She spoke as she took my hand and led me to the corner of the room towards the balcony. "I have nothing to say."

She frowned deeply at my reply. "You have to be strong. I have made sure Lidia goes with you as your primary lady-in-waiting." I looked at my mother with relief but shook my head.

"No she is my only friend, I cannot take her there. Mother, it's dangerous-"

My mother shook her head," She insisted and it is decided-"

Before we both could speak we heard the main doors open and The king and Queen were announced. We bowed to them as they walked through the crowd and walked toward the front. As the King spoke, I felt like I couldn't focus. I was staring at the ground for what felt like seconds when my mother tapped on my shoulder. She frowned at me, questioning with her brows if I was alright, but I shook my head.

I looked around to see all of the people had gone silent. It was as if I could hear the wind outside, I was trying to find a reason when the doors of the entrance opened. It was them. I couldn't see much because of our position, but one of the King's guards walked towards me and bowed I knew it was time.

"The King has asked for your presence in the library Madam."

I gulp. I turned to find the man who would be marrying me but I was too far away. As The King and Queen welcomed their guests I was taken to the back leaving my mother behind.

‖ CHAPTER 3 ‖

I clutched my thin shawl and walked to the library. As I waited in that familiar room yet again my tears just seemed to run free. But I wipe them off soon enough. It felt like I was in that room for hours, as I walked around tracing my fingers against the several thick books on the shelves I made my way to the large window behind the desk and watched the clear sky.

The loud thump and opening of the door made me jump and turn around to see the King and my father.

"Ruby Williams."

As the King called my name I picked up my dress and hurried from behind the desk. And before I could question him I saw someone walk in through the doors.

It was him. Of course, I could just tell.

Dark hair, a thick beard, sharp eyes, and a defined jawline. His frame was larger than the knights who fought in the war. His muscular frame was covered with his black and grey attire. I noticed how his one hand rested on the sword held over his hip. If eyes could kill quietly, I would be dead.

And when they did not literally kill someone, one felt the overwhelming urge to kill themselves. I felt as if I was in danger just being in that one space with him.

He was part human, like us. But humans could never carry such a dangerous aura as he did. He carried himself with pride. But to us, it looked as if a dangerous animal stalking its prey.

My body suddenly filled with heat as if I was on fire, I was confused, and feeling weak. Perhaps it was the wine.

But my quick reaction to his entrance was to bend my knees and bow to the Lycan King as if I were bound to it. One has to show respect to rulers but they never feel such pressure from inside. To the King and Queen, I did it out of respect, but to King Xerxes, I felt pressure, like I had my head under a sword if I chose not to.

Snapping away from my thoughts and how I felt, I kept my eyes on the ground and stayed in my position unaware of what I had to do.

I for some reason felt as If our King himself feared something. Not King Xerxes, he wasn't as cowardly but perhaps he feared what King Xerxes might do. Never mind what the King felt! I was shaking with fear myself.

I peeked at the man but my eyes never traveled past his chest as my father lent me his hand to help me up. But I never accepted it. I rose from my position and never uttered a word. Nor did he.

"We hope our agreement produces good benefits for both our kingdoms." My father spoke softly and with a low shakey voice.

It seemed like the air inside this library just vanished. As I struggled to breathe my hand pressed below my breasts and I looked around for some escape.

"You need some air." He spoke for the first time. His voice wasn't as rough or harsh as I thought it would be. Instead, it was something like husky, soft but stern. And I did not understand how he noticed me half suffocating.

"Shall we dine?" The King filled the sudden silence between us four and my father nodded before walking to the doors. As the doors opened, I felt much better. The strong lights of the halls filled the space as much as they could and the air suddenly lifted.

The guards bowed as the King walked past them and Fred stood waiting to escort me. As I made my way across King Xerxes my body weakened, I felt like I would faint like a weak lady. As I reached my hand to place it over Fred's forearm a sudden warm wind brushed from behind me and my hand rested upon another arm.

A series of sudden shivers run down my body.

King Xerxes had put himself between me and Fred and before we both could register I was being escorted out to the ballroom by the Lycan King himself.

It was such a pressuring moment, as all turned to us and bowed to the Two Kings. My breathing became shallow. We made our way to the balcony, I noticed my father sitting beside me and King Xerxes on the other side of me. I never hated my father as much. I felt like running away, not from the ball but away from my father.

King Xerxes stayed quiet, his companion whispering some things to him once in a while and earning his nod. I took a sip of the wine in front of me and pressed my hand over my chest as my breathing suddenly became faster.

"Excuse me, I need to use the powder room," I stated before attempting to stand up but the big chair refused to move. I felt my chair being pushed back and I got to see Fred. For some reason, Fred's presence helped me calm down. I hardly knew this man yet, his quiet aura made me feel better than my own father's.

I moved from the balcony to the back rooms and the maids followed me I creased my eyebrows.

"No, I want to be left alone," I stated with a stern voice.

As I freshened myself and walked out, Fred stood beside the doors waiting for me. I just stare at the doors which lead back to the table and sigh. My lips frown as I look around and press my hands on my stomach. Whether it was my tight dress, my utterly upset stomach, or my poor ability to eat much at all, it was making me feel weak. I felt cold but hot at the same time.

"Are you not well Madam?"

I looked up at Fred and shook my head.

"Your shawl." He extended his hand and I grabbed my shawl wrapping it around my shoulders.

"Is there anywhere I can just sit, I need to get away and rest."

He frowned, his eyes turned to the doors to the balcony, contemplating what to do before he sighed and nodded down at me.

"This way-" He steps aside pointing his hand towards the left of the hall.

"The painting gallery is just ahead, I will let the Queen's lady-in-waiting know are resting here."

I smiled as I walked to the gallery and opened the large doors. The dim light hall of painting was like a never-ending cave.

"Thank you, Fred. I won't take long."

I entered the hall and slowly walked inside as he left the doors open and walked away to let the Queen know. I look around and keep my shawl on the console table next to the door.

I felt scared, alone in such a grand hall with nobody to talk with. I walked along the dimly lit chandeliers while observing the paintings and feeling better slowly. I take a deep breath but the bodice of this gown was laced much more tightly. Having no desire to call for help I bite my lip inch my hands closer to the ribbon on the lower back of my waist and untie it.

I could just ask the maid to redo it when I go back out. I undid the laces bit by bit just enough to loosen the bust but not fall and sighed in happiness as the bodice got just a bit loser. Just enough for me to breathe. I huff walking a bit further down the path and stare at one particular painting of a woman holding pearls. My eyes fixed on her name, "Amelia-" I whispered.

She was the King's mother. He resembled her greatly.

Through my eye's peripheral vision, I see a shadow stand between the two large doors. The light from the back cast a shadow over their face. I stayed unfazed as I knew it would be Fred. But something in me told me not to look. I suddenly felt cornered, alone but with someone with a strong presence. I chose to ignore it as It was surely the wine on my empty stomach. I keep my hand under my bust and rub my thumb over my corset.

I see him entering the Hall and sigh turning around. I thought of Fred as a brother, There was no need for me to cover my back with undid laces and furthermore, my maid was always my second escort. There was no need for me to question his actions as I had learned to trust him through this first week.

"Is everyone jolly out there? Of course, they would, why would they care about some Duke's lonely daughter." I let my thoughts get the better of me and spoke out of turn.

But I received no answer back. Fred wasn't a talker, to begin with.

I sighed looking up at the painting.

"I am dying to go back and sleep," I whispered.

The feeling of a finger brushing lightly over my laces caught me off guard. It wasn't something a touch could do. I felt chills run up my spine and my heartbeat quickened its pace in seconds. I jumped and turned around stepping back only to find King Xerxes towering over my little frame.

‖ Chapter 4 ‖

My knees weakened and I gave a curtsey immediately. My stomach turned in twists as the proximity was far too close for me to handle. He did something to my body that I could not understand. The fear I felt was incredible.

"Rise."

I stayed as I was, even after the command was given. I felt if I stood up, I would fall back again with the blood rushing to my head, me fainting was inevitable.

"Are you deaf?" He asked and I lifted my head shaking it and slowly stood up.

My hands coming together and my fingers, trembling, fidgeting together.

"Y-your Majesty-" My words faded into a whisper and I wondered how they addressed their King. Their customs might be very different from ours.

He stared down at me, sort of observing my clumsy self wondering why I was even given as a treaty. There was nothing good in me. As they all said, I was only a good enough face. When I saw his finger inch closer to me I wanted to step back, I almost gasped as he grabbed a strand of my hair as it lay right over my softly heaving chest. He pulled my strand and stared at it.

Was it him? or his kind that made us humans feel so afraid and highly sensitive to their touch? I felt my legs clench together and heat rushed from below my gut to my body. My neck could be burning as well. I could imagine how embarrassing my flushed red face was. I was wondering with a hundred questions what he was doing. My thin white skin would turn red at the slightest heat. It was embarrassing.

"I see you are afraid of me like most."

My nervous tongue let loose like in most situations.

"Most? Your Majesty, I think all do."

I slapped myself at such an indecorous comment. How could I say that? Was it the wine? No, It was just my nerves. No, NO It WAS the wine.

"Not all-" He muttered and I saw him walk towards the painting, looking up at it, he was right beside me, our hands almost touching.

"Some only fear seeing the ones who never did die."

I gulp slowly looking at him and lowering my gaze.

"Do y-you kill a lot of- people?" I asked.

He lowered his gaze and turned to me, his gaze made me suffocate all over again. His eyes looked as if they were filled with rage forever. I could not look him in his eyes for more than a second. As I dropped my gaze he spoke.

"I don't kill Ruby, my assassins do."

There it was, dizziness overcoming my body. I felt so hot I could faint.

"You do not look well" He stated, his hand pressed against my lower back and I stopped myself from gasping out loud.

I felt a burning tingling feeling right there. I couldnt hold myself up anymore as my knees gave in and I stumbled back and bent my knees to fall down but he pulled me up by tightening his hand around me.

A soft gasp escapes my lips as my hand rests upon his large biceps. I was so small in comparison to him, our heights weren't far different but our frames surely were. It didn't take him much effort to stop my falling body and hold me up with one hand pressed to my back. My eyes met his as he glanced down once before coming up to my eyes again.

"Forgive me," I said softly but when I tried to get out of his hold he did not let me.

I jump slightly as his both hands wrap around my lower back.

What was he doing? Here? In the gallery? Was he trying to touch me before our marriage?

My questions were soon thrown out the window as he took both ends of my bodice and tightened them. I kept my frozen stated and shocked eyes on his chest and he tied the laces together and stepped back.

"I would not like my wife roaming the halls of another castle with her laces undone. Get back to the table after your maid has tended to your needs, Ruby."

His voice....I want to hear it again.

I could comprehend all the things I was feeling. As he left the room, my maid and Fred looked at him. I blinked and walked out to the hall.

"Are you alright Miss? You look flushed." Glenda, one of the maids serving the Queen asked.

I nodded.

Glenda fixed me up before I made my way back to the ballroom. I sat down and took a sip of the wine before having a few bites of the food on my plate. Before I knew it the dances had begun. I stared at the floor below and watched in awe as the beautiful ball gowns all ladies glittered on the dance floor.

As I take a sip of wine I suddenly cough and set the glass down putting the lapcloth over my mouth. I see his hand grab a glass of water from the other side and set it before me. I grab it and drown the glass quickly.

I realized I had three glasses of wine-something I never drink. Wait....I had two before. How could I possibly hold myself up anymore?

So was the wine a reason I was feeling so lightheaded and sleepy?

King Xerxes suddenly stood up making us all stand up as an act of respect. The King and Queen stood up slowly and he looked down at me. I look at his hand and him again before grabbing it. I had no idea what he was doing or where we were going as he dragged me down the floor and into the ballroom. People stopped their dance as I was escorted to the middle of the floor.

My worst nightmare or my dream. It was one of those. At my now broken marriage, I imagined myself dancing under the golden chandelier with Price Edward. But I wondered how I feel about thinking of him now. As I placed my hand over the King's shoulder but it falls to his bicep and the other was in his, I suddenly felt as if people were judging me. I looked around softly as we took the floor with a slow dance and my heartbeat quickened its pace. Between the crowd stood Edward, watching me dance.

But my attention was suddenly diverted to the King as his hand wrapped around my waist tight.

"I hear you were betrothed to another."

My eyes snapped at him and my tongue caught up. I feared if I avoided his question or lied, I would be in far more danger than if the truth was told.

So I nodded slowly, "Yes, It was broken after the treaty."

"Did you love that man?"

"No, your Majesty." maybe lies weren't as bad sometimes.

"I do not like liars. Usually, they just get tortured but you stay my exception, Ruby."

I had the most fearful chills in my body as I saw his eyes, did they change? Yes. They did look even more terrifying than before somehow. yes. And I could see with no questions that King Xerxes was not a human I could hold a good conversation with. It was better my voice stayed silent with him around and for the rest of my life as I live, I will half to hold myself back from all pleasure of freedom as I marry him.

As I was escorted to the dining table, I noticed how people never looked him in the eyes. I realized I did so. My mind was filled with questions about my actions. Which one of my actions might have offended him? Or might be offending to their kind in general?

As we walked up the stairs for a sudden talk as the King ordered Fred to pass on his message I struggled to walk up the stairs with my dress. I stepped over my own petticoat and stumbled back on the stairs to avoid falling on my face. I wasn't as worried because Fred was right behind me but my eyes opened wide as King Xerxes turned round in a flash of light as grabbed me by my waist. If that didn't get a gasp out of my mouth, his pulling me roughly into his hard chest made me do so.

He spoke nothing but stopped Fred with his eyes as Fred tried to help me stand straight. He looked behind us to the maid who ran past Fred and held my hand before King Xerxes felt us walk further up the stairs.

"Are you alright Miss? Forgive me-"

"No, it's fine." I cut her off and looked at Fred who was now in front of me blocking the guard's view of me and letting the maid adjust my dress.

"Forgive me," I whispered walking onto the balcony and bowing to the King and Queen before walking further and standing beside my father as both the Kings sat on the couch behind the table.

"Leave us." Said The Queen.

"You to Sir Williams." The king muttered taking a swing of the brown liquid in his glass.

My father looked at me once before bowing and leaving us.

I felt King Xerxes stare at me and my heart suddenly started beating heavily. There was such an awkward silence for a long time as the music in the ballroom echoed in the background.

"I shall be blunt." The king finally spoke as he glanced at the Queen once.

King Xerxes sat there, his hand on the head of the couch and the other holding the glass of alcohol, his stare looked as if he was debating but with anger.

"My niece, Ruby is incapable of becoming a Queen. A queen to your kind."

That hurt but it was true. I look at King Xerxes but his expression remains neutral. I looked down in embarrassment as the King spoke of the truth.

|| **Chapter 5** ||

"She is weak, fragile, and had never been involved in politics. Her studies were only based on geographic and history subjects. She might just be the worst wife and Queen in history."

I never realized how I stood there like a defeated girl with tears around my eyes realizing that I never accomplished anything in my life.

" A king will always choose his people over his loved ones. And as I do that I ask of you to not expect much from her but treat her well. She only had us to speak for her and now she has no one."

My tears started rolling down my eyes as the king said his last words.

"I understand your words quite well Alexander. You are making sure I don't send her back."

That hurt even more.

"But one thing we do not do in our Kingdom-" He leaned forward keeping his elbows on his legs and staring at the King, "- is let another man speak for our wife. We believe she has her own voice-" He said standing up and so did The king and Queen.

He proceeded to light a cigar and puff out the smoke glancing down at the dancing crowd.

"And this is the last time I shall tolerate any man speaking for my future wife because from tomorrow she is going to be the Queen of my kingdom. And I do not like anyone berating my Wife, not even her prior King.

"But one thing we do not do in our Kingdom is, let another man speak for our wife. We believe she has her own voice-" He said standing up and so did The king and Queen. He proceeded to light a cigar and puff out the smoke glancing down at the dancing crowd.

"And this is the last time I shall tolerate any man speaking for my future wife because from tomorrow she is going to be the Queen of my kingdom. And I do not like anyone berating my queen, not even her prior King."

Tomorrow? But the wedding is next week-

I stare at King Xerxes as he looked at me. My eyes were still filled with tears as he walked towards me. My legs felt weak as I hold on to the head of the couch and look down, something I found myself doing when he came closer.

"I hope I see you in something better than just plain white my wife." He whispered as his face came inches near me. I could smell that musky scent as his beard lightly rubbed over my cheek and his lips laid on my ears for mere seconds before he pulled away. He nodded once at the king before leaving us be.

I fell on my bed the minute that dress was off me and my hair had been freed from the tight pins and clips. I could only think about what would happen to me as I left this kingdom. King Xerxes was not a man one would even speak around and here I was, going to be in his bed and around him. And If I was hated just enough, I would be locked up and never to see the light of day again.

And as I closed my eyes his face suddenly flashed across the darkness making my heart suddenly race.

[Xerxes Lycan]

As I heard about the Duke's daughter I wanted to hang that man by his throat. Trading a human to be my wife so my soldiers don't invade their forests? What cowards. I had little knowledge about those royals, but I never thought they would put their women at such low trades.

"We will not engage in a fight but we will have our reserves build up on our sides of the land," said Andrew on my behalf. The duke bowed his head and left. I thought of breaking the treaty quite many times. This was why I paid a visit to King Alexander, to break off a treaty with no foundation or basis and have a fair fight or surrender to me if they wished to cherish their mere ten thousand soldiers.

It was afternoon as I walked into the private chambers of the castle. I stare out to the gardens and notice her. I could not take my eyes off her. There was the reason my wolf suddenly pounced up and growled at the man behind that girl. She was making haste towards the inner court holding up her maroon dress.

My jaw clenched as the glass in my fingers suddenly broke.

"My King." Andrew walked to me. I could feel him sense my glare and move his eyes to where I stare.

"It can't be"

"Find out about her. I need to answers, now!"

I ordered him as he ran out.

I could not let go of the constant urge to break all and everything in that chamber and run toward her but I was holding myself back. If these people should want their limbs intact then the King better give me what truly belongs to me. And she did.

I tap my finger on the glass of scotch as I wait for Andrew and as time passes by my anger and frustration could not be held back. What if my mate was married? My wolf growled in anger. Then there was nothing to be done but kill that man.

"Sir." The doors slammed open and I stare at him waiting for him to speak up.

"Well!?" My voice echoed through the walls.

Andrew grinned, "Ruby Diego Williams, youngest daughter of Duke Aiden Williams. She is the one the duke promised."

I stood up, the amount of happiness through this small coincidence was through the roof. I could not imagine letting her be with anyone other than her mate, Me.

"You should know Sir, that she was apparently engaged, To Prince Edward. Their engagement was canceled after our treaty was made."

She was to be another man's wife. It infuriated me. To think, these 35 years of my life I never had a mate and now, she was nearly taken away from me. No, absolutely not.

"We are agreeing to this arrangement."

Andrew bowed, "I will do the necessary." and he left.

To think my mate was innocent, beautiful, so far away from me but a human, gave me more reason to keep her protected.

As I wait to be introduced to my queen I make haste towards the library. I could see the struggle of these humans keeping up to our long strides. I laugh in my mind as Andrew chuckles at one scared guard who held the door. As they opened, there she was, in my presence finally.

I could feel her fear and sorrow. I wondered if it was because her previous engagement was broken, it angered me too much but the thought she was be with me soon help me take my frustrations back. She was my soulmate, she would understand soon.

While Humans did not have as much sixth sense as we did, in terms of a bond, they find out soon enough. Especially if their mate is the Alpha.

She was scared, bowing down the minute I entered, I suppose she felt the bond the minute I walked in. The way I could feel her heart beat fasten its pace, I knew she already submitted herself to me. However, the lack of jewels in her neck exposed her beautiful milky skin. My hands clenched with absolute furry as I realised most men could see her exposed cleavage. When she bowed to me, my eyes fell on her heaving chest. He hands were trembling and she was flushed red. Her beautiful milky white hair hung down to her waist covered with pearls.

I appuad the ladies for dressing up my mate in red, a colour which looked so beautiful on her. I bet she refused to wear the pearls I sent her in order to stay elegant. I smirked in my head.

I couldn't wait to touch her, feel her, kiss her, run my fingers through her beautiful hair and most importantly mark that pretty bare neck first so no human could ever look at her in the eyes again.

When she walked away to use the powder room I couldn't help but worry. This was something I feared the most, letting her be free and leave without a guard I trusted and heavily worrying. After a couple of minutes had passed I couldn't help myself but leave to go talk with her.

I needed to hear her voice. I needed to see her eyes which she so smartly avoided showing me.

And when I saw her guard Fredrick standing at the doors of the gallery I couldn't help but feel as if I should dismiss him. But she could get scared easily. People run to the only hope they have if scared. If I dismissed the man who had been accompanying her since the start of this agreement for her own safety then she would find it cruel.

When I entered the dark halls of the painting gallery my heart stopped as I saw my queen's laces undone, she stood quite staring at a painting and I was ready to kill anyone who had done something. I was ready to command Andrew when I saw her little hands trying to let lose her laces herself. She huffed closing her eyes with a little frown on her face as she kept her hand on her chest breathing slowly. ----When she looked at me, I could swear I felt my blood rush down where it wasn't supposed to. Those indecent thoughts of her in bed, my hands over her, and just us. I held my neutral posture as my shield to avoid letting loose and grabbing her.

No...Back off..she is far more elegant and innocent than I thought.

I sigh, making sure her dressed was tied up again before we walked out. And when she danced with me, I couldn't help but feel the pressure of everyone watching us. Not just the men, but the women too. They thought of me as a beast and I was, but for her, never. And it was a shame my mate would take some time to understand why we are like this, possessive, protective, far too dangerous than humans. But if she accepted me, I would spare nothing. If she didn't I would have no other choice than to claim her forcefully.

‖ CHAPTER 6 ‖

There was nothing my mind could think of but how terrible that pure white piece of cloth looked on me.

"I hope I see you in something better than just plain white, Ruby."

I look away and closed my eyes before looking back again. No, I wasn't considering this colour bad because of what he said. It just looked terrible. But what else would a woman being wed wear?

"Take it off."

The seamstress frowned as she took the fabric off me and I stepped down from the pedestal huffing in frustration and taking a sip of water.

"You do not like the fabric?" My mother asked.

I look at her, her poor face in frown probably thinking I was displeased with her choice of dress. Her hands stopped knitting the new sweater she meant to make for me this coming winter. Her brows were creased and her lips were in a pout.

"No mum, It's not the fabric I-I can't see me in such a blinding white cloth."

My mother, unsure of what I meant, looked at the seamstress. The well-known seamstress, Madam Molly, someone who was trusted by the queen as she sowed many of her gowns stood in question as no woman had ever hated white for her own wedding.

"But, white is a must, It symbolizes-"

"My purity?" I cut my mother off and stare at her with my brows raised mocking the meaning.

My mother chuckled rolling her eyes and keeping that half-knitted sweater down.

"Yes, It does but there is more to it. It symbolizes the beginning of a new life, good fortune, white can be tainted but it can never be forgotten-"

I had no idea what she meant by that, to be honest. I just look back at the mirror standing in my petticoat and sigh.

"Would you please find a fabric less, white?"

Madam Molly raised her eyebrows at me as if to find my request preposterous and nodded before leaving the room.

"Are those-" my mother's finger pointed towards the three boxes kept at the table at the end of the bed.

"I received them from Sir Fred, they are sent by King Xerxes." I stare at it and remember what Sir Fred told me.

"The two below are yours," I said looking at the laces the maid gave me for my new petticoats and she looked at me in question.

My eyes linger over the soft cream lace before returning to my mother's wide eyes My mother slowly walked towards the boxes and opens the topmost box, sitting over the two below. I see her looking at what was inside then keeping the topmost box aside and opening the ones below.

I had not touched them for I had no interest in jewels, in fact, I thought I looked ridiculous in them.

"Goodness, do they expect us to accept this and be happy that my daughter is entering the realm of vicious creatures? how degraded and gullible do they think we are ?"

I spoke nothing about what my mother commented. I did not think of them as any different than us but she was right to think they were a danger to me as a human. It was the truth. And to the think, I was to stand next to their king.

Was I going be a disappointment to his subjects or was I going to be the target of mockery?

Words against the King can be punished but a foreign Queen? What protected me? Nothing...

"Why are you staring at that like you have seen a ghost-" My words were caught in my tongue as I saw the contents of those three boxes.

Rubies, Saffire, diamonds, emeralds, gold, and....pearls.

Carcanet's, lockets, pendants, brooches, watches, and more pearls..I t looked so magnificent yet so disgusting.

I chuckled at the jewels and diamonds in the box and then they were a crest. A title was given to my folks to give them permission to enter the fort of their lands on my behalf. Not the castle, just the fort.

"They really think of me as an object mother." I chuckled as she held my hand.

"How dare they think of us like peasants, did the king not offer a good enough treaty in your place that you should now be compared to gems? Petty Objects owned by men, never to be free once claimed, I will send them back, I will not accept any form of bribes-" as my mother turned around but immediately kneeled on the ground in shock, My eyes followed her actions to see the Queen standing at the doors of my temporary chamber.

I gulp giving the queen a curtsey before standing back up. My mother stayed on the ground recognizing her crime of speaking ill of our King.

"Forgive me your highness I spoke out of the tongue."

The queen smiled, "You may rise duchess I understand your anger but, these are traditions. One cannot ignore it. Do not take it as an insult. It was quite gallant of the King to even send such jewels, I heard their traditions may be different but at least they respected ours."

"Forgive me, my Queen, I cannot stop thinking of how I will survive."

"I understand, which is why I am sending one of my own maids with your ladies on waiting and Knight. Any trouble, she will let me know"

I look down at my useless self.

"I-I regret to decline your highness for these decisions. I cannot have you watching over me all the time. I am on my own and I should be capable enough to handle myself. I have Lydia, Sir Fredrick. They will let you know of my well-being"

The queen's lips turned into a proud smile and she nodded.

"Spoken like a Lady and to be a Queen. I shall see you in the court by 5"

I blink at her as she turned around to leave.

"Court?" I asked and she stopped.

"You have to sign the paper my dear." She stated turning to me.

"Paper?" I asked

"The treaty papers. You have to sign them and officially be announced as being betrothed To the King. Those papers will give you the title of a Lady to be...The Queen"

"Oh, I never knew about this."

The queen frowned looking at my mother, "Your father was supposed to let you know before noon today. I suppose he is caught up in work. I shall send your maid in to prepare you."

***

I hang my head low in disappointment. My father refused to even see me after that ball night. When I should be the one ignoring him.

Our heels clicked the echoing hallway as I made my way towards the court. My eyes land on the man who stood with King Xerxes. The man in charge of witnessing my signature was Andrew Lycan. Although I heard he took a different title name, he bowed at me and I give a nod of appreciation to him while I walk towards the end of the court.

The King, Queen, my folks, and some important court subjects stood at the end staring at me. I felt like I would burn under those gazes. And I stood there for ages as it felt when my eyes landed again on Sir Andrew.

I could not understand how he looked much more intimidating than the King himself. There was something about werewolves. Perhaps it was the witnessed actions by humans that continued the fear through humankind, we might never witness their real form, but as our ancestors saw, we knew what they were capable of.

Their eyes always carried that particular aura of standing with a purpose. Not zoning out like us, always being a step ahead. Highly aware of their surroundings and the people surrounding them. One move and they were alert. I did not know this, it was what my folks told me about them when I was a child. And that I had seen a man truly from their side, I could tell it was true. No doubts.

"Ruby." My father's voice echoed through the hollow court and I snapped my head up to him.

He extended his hand for me to grab while walking towards me. I took my time staring into his soft eyes. I loved my father's eyes, they were green and brown, I always envied the way they looked at my mother. I wished for a man to look at me the same way.

"Come, my dear." He whispered and I took his hand still staring at his face. Yes, I loathed him but I did not want to forget his face after I left for good.

Now that I think of it, he could've been killed as well if the treaty did not offer any good price. And The king would hate him for losing the negotiation possibly sending us into a low-rank title and out of this castle ground.

I give a furstrated sigh as I look at the papers spread across the huge oak table.

The priest hands me the pen and I breathe out looking at Sir Andrew who was closest to me to ask where my signature was required. He quickly stepped up and pointed to the small line at the end of the page where a large beautiful confusing signature of King Xerxes lay. It was such a difficult signature that no man could ever redo it.

I didn't think much when I signed it. I stepped back and gave the pen to the King's hand who signed below it as my witness.

There, it was done. I was The Lycan King's wife. And from now, my freedom was good as gone.

I had such fear and stress as they prepared me for the wedding that morning. I blink away some tears several times as I fussed around. I had some tea, but the feeling of an empty stomach coupled with anxiety could wear the toughest man alive. My hand shook and my legs were going numb.

I stare at the bouquet and frown, I thought I had requested them to put sage in it.

"There must be a mistake, My daughter requested the sage to be put in it."

The sage was in our grandmother's memory. But maybe here is where they start suppressing my requests. It was going to happen soon away. The florist bowed before apologizing.

"Forgive me Madam, but I was told no sight of sage should be seen.

I snap my head toward him in confusion.

"What are the creatures afraid of sage ?"

The room fell silent as my mother made a very offensive statement. Speaking in such a way could lead you down the dungeons. I frown at my mother.

" We cannot even put our memory in this wedding." She whispered leaving the bridal chamber.

I sigh looking around ashamed until my eyes settled on the mirror, myself. Me in a champagne white, and cream lace. I had a teardrop pearl and ruby necklace and that was all I wore in my mother's memory.

"Madam." called my maid and opened the doors. I peek outside at the guards and see my father waiting with Sir Andrew.

As I step out they both snapped their heads at me. It was unexpected for Sir Andrew to bow to me out of respect. Flustered I gave a curtsey but he stepped forward.

"From now on, You only curtsey to Kings and Queen, Madam." He stated before gesturing for me to take my father's hand.

I felt the room closing in on me as we walked to the cathedral. I wanted to run away. I wanted to talk to someone. Cry a little. But there I stood, waiting for the door to open.

"Deep breath. Don't let them see your head low." My father whispered and I look up taking a deep breath.

All I could say when the doors opened, was that I saw a man, at the end of the aisle who was looking at me. While the others stared, his brows were creased. And somehow my first thought was.

What is King Xerxes worried about?

‖CHAPTER 7‖

Before I knew it I was standing right in front of him. My eyes could not meet his, not because of a slight height difference but because I just could not look him in the eyes. I feared it would anger him.

My hands trembled as my father took my hand and placed it over his hands. And I will never exaggerate how that felt. Like warmth but with a shock in my body. I noticed him staring at me for just over a minute before looking at the priest.

The priest was the only man who could look at King Xerxes in the eyes as he said his prayers for us. He was the only man I saw, who did not hold fear in his eyes as the Lycan King stood before him.

As we faced each other, he took my other hand. I didn't even notice the slight trembles my hands gave away.

I felt a sense of ending as he put a ring on my finger. It was such a simple, elegant ring. Gold and thin with three small diamonds. As I hold the ring I pray to god I don't drop it. I hurried to put it on his finger for fear of messing up.

As the priest blessed us and announced us as man and wife, I gulp as his hand wrapped around my waist very lightly. So lightly I could feel his fingers tracing my back. His lips lightly laid on my lips for only a moment but all I saw were warm lights as I closed my eyes.

My lips tingled as he pulled away and took my hand. We bowed to the lord once before leaving for the door.

There was no feast here. There was just me giving a final full curtsey to the King and Queen before having the time to say goodbye to my family and then I was whisked away to the carriage but not before a quick bath and other ablutions with a brief change into a simpler cream gown for the long travel. I was thankful I got the time to refresh myself, I did not want two days of travel with no proper bath and bathroom break and me on my heels to get there.

I smile at Sir Fred as he prepared his horse and he bowed towards me as I walk to him.

"I will be taking a different route to the Kingdom Madam. I hope I see in a span of two days if the weather allows it" I frown.

"But, why?"

He was the only man I could trust.

"I have to make haste and get to the court before your Highness so as to deal with all the necessary requirements like your personal needs, how the court works and what your, The Queen's duty will be. It would be easier for me to cross the mountains from the east. Unfortunately, the carriage cannot pass such narrow hills so you have to go through the longer route."

I frown and he looked behind me towards Sir Andrew and back at me.

"Do not worry Madam. You will be protected by six soldiers and The King himself. Lydia will be with you at all times."

I sigh nodding.

"I worry for you, not myself"

Sir Fred gave a light chuckle, "Madam, there is no need to worry. The route I will take is a safe one at that and I will have a companion for half of it".

I smile, assured them that he would be fine. For I need him to make sure I was on my best behavior back on the court and I needed him for he was the only man from back home who the Queen trusted. I said my final goodbye before walking to the carriage.

As I sit down and make myself comfortable assuming I was the only one in the carriage as the footman closed the door. I rub my hands together as the cold weather has descended early this season. The door opened catching me by surprise. My eyes went wide as a hawk when King Xerxes stepped in and took a seat facing me. I lower my head a second nature to my reaction.

He looked at me once before calling for a servant and saying something in a language I did not understand. We wait a while in silence till the man came back with a thick blue shawl and handed it to the King.

He placed it over my lap and closed the door knocking once and I saw Sir Andrew get on his horse.

"We take the route from Greenstake's?" He asked and King Xerxes nodded.

"It will be colder as we move up the mountain. I expect your lady's maid packed a coat for the journey?"

His Voice...

That was my first thought, It was so rough and manly but there was that hint of softness to it. perhaps just my thought. His voice ..might I dare say can be compared to warmth but with fire underneath which could blaze through the firewood anytime and burn someone too close.

After my mind was content with comparing the King's voice to many things I realized I was asked a question. And It reminded me of my maid. Who had no apprehension of the weather up in the mountains to the south or north and had never been told what type of clothing to carry for the travel.

I sat there with my half-open mouth petrified to speak and disappoint or worse anger the King. So I gulp down the fear and shook my head.

"Forgive me, I-I -" Why should I take the blame for myself? I am her mistress, It was entirely Lydia's fault, yes?

"My maid did not -"

He looked at me with a quizzical brow before nodding and looking away. Soon I realized he has some papers in his hands which he continued reading and browsing through for half the journey, while, I was in agony.

I could not keep my eyes off his hands or face or hair. It was just impossible for a man to be so perfect looking. Well, perfection always comes with some disappointment. I expected it to be his attitude toward me.

A thought dawned on me. I was a human in their land. He could very well toss me in a chamber locked away and have his mistress with him. Oh, the sorrow it may give me.

The carriage came to a sudden halt which sends me jerking forward and right into his extended arms. His brows creased in worry or anger maybe? his hands stayed on my arm while my hand fell on his chest to stop my face from bumping into it all at once.

"What is it?" He asked looking out. His one hand pulled away the curtains of the carriage but the other stayed on my forearm. I retract my hand from his chest, my cheeks clearly flushed and I in embarrassed as the footman inquired about the sudden halt.

"Apologies Your Majesty. A minor delay-"

"For what?" King Xerxes questions the footman. So it was anger indeed.

"A body. Human." Said Sir Andrew as he walked past our carriage.

|| CHAPTER 8||

The blunt and straight explanation of the situation wasn't expected. I suppose these people do not waste time thinking about how to speak in a softer manner. It intrigued me.

I look out slightly as the King stepped out.

I follow his body as he walks ahead and with him everybody else. I should say in such situations if it were our King, he wouldn't be told about such a situation or refrained from stepping out as it may be a trap. But here, it was the King who always stepped first.

My curious mind couldn't get enough as I stepped out of the carriage on the dirt road. Trees guiding both sides and towering over us.

"Your highness-"I turn around to see a young soldier on his horse.

"Please stay back, it is a gruesome scene."

Well, I have had my share of blood and wounds watching the sword fights in court. I look back and step forward. There laid that body of a poor soul between the six soldiers, our footmen. Sir Andrew and the King examining it.

I could only see the head but when some of the soldiers moved my gut fell. My heart felt like it would beat out of my chest and my stomach filled with fear. I held a gasp back as my eyes could not take in what I saw.

King Xerxes, as if he knew already lifted his gaze directly to my eyes and watched me.

That man's eyes, tongue, and hand were missing, torn off. Legs twisted to the other side. Guts spilled and the neck was cut open with dried blood covering the brown soil.

"Not a bear attack Sir. Not even a normal wolf, It was-" The soldier who had finished examining the body looked up at Sir Andrew whose eyes were on me.

In fact, everyone's eyes were on me as I stood there breathing heavily as panic set in.

Blood I had seen but this, I never could imagine. I was terrified. My arms started trembling slightly as the King walked past the men towards me shielding my view from that.

"Get back in the carriage Ruby."

He did not have to tell me twice as I obey in an instant and turn around. My hand stayed on my chest, trying to calm my heart down. My eyes look at the soldier who had now gotten off his horse, he had a face of worry as he looked at me. My eyes shake looking around and I looked toward the tree line once to look at something better like the green color before sitting when I saw something.

I stare at it for a minute before two hands wrapped around my waist scaring me. I gasp turning just a little to realize it was the King. A slight relief washes my eyes. Something in his touch calmed me down. He moved his one hand to settle right under my chest and the other touched my shaky palm.

Highly aware of his warm hand right under my highly sensitive breasts I tried my best to point at that thing that looked like a bag in the bushes.

"Uh, um. There is a b-bag?" I stutter. That bloody sight is still in my mind.

King Xerxes snapped his head to my finger pointing in a direction.

On the command of his eyes, the soldier standing before us walked towards that thing and pulled it out of the bushes.

"Carriage, now."

That wasn't the soft voice I felt before. It was a command and this time I go back in the carriage and King Xerxes closed the door walking back ahead.

I sit there for what felt like hours as they moved that poor man. A small knock made me flinch and I open the window to Sir Andrew handing me a bottle of water.

"Thank you."

I take a few sips before handing it back and giving a long sigh. I scoot to the edge of the seat and lean my body and head on the wall of the carriage looking at the trees and thinking about this to distract myself. My eyes fall on the hem of my dress. My cream gown, and possibly my second wedding dress had dirt over its hem. I sigh taking my kerchief and dusting it off but it only reminded me of that gruesome body.

I give up leaning back on that wall. And when the door opened again, King Xerxes said something before sitting and closing the door. The carriage moved as we pass over that soil which had a body just minutes ago. I was sure they did something. The time they took to move the body and find a local villager was enough to ensure it.

But I asked no questions.

"Ruby."

I wish he did not call me by my name. It made me melt slightly.

"Yes, your highness?" I whispered looking at him but not at his eyes.

"Are you feeling unwell?" He asked in a stern voice. His demeanor seemed sort of serious. And I worried if any word of mine might anger him more.

"No, Your Majesty, I am fine-"

I watch in fear as he got up slightly before moving my dress aside and sitting next to me. I stare at him as he put his hand behind my head and my heart almost beat out of my ribcage. My stomach flipped as his hand wedged between my shoulder and that wall then pulled my body to lean over his.

"It's just Xerxes to you when we are alone," he whispered in my ear and I felt as if my legs trembled at that moment.

Oh, they did tremble, for the way he whispered. But Somewhere in my mind, I was scared of him. Scared of his cruel demeanor and his real nature. I was scared of offending the King. I felt as if I had no right to even look him in the eye or touch him or speak to him.

His hand left my shoulder and setting on the head of the seat as I sat there with my head on his shoulder.

I didn't think he would even touch me.

As we sat in silence I finally dozed off. But once in a while when the carriage hit a dirt road I would wake up slightly but keep my closed to go back to sleep. I completely forgot I was sleeping on the King as I adjusted my head twice.

Suddenly I was lifted from my seat and I gasp as he settled me between his legs with my legs hanging over his thigh.

I search for questions or answers as he leaned back flustered and blushing red.

"I assume this might be more comfortable for you to sleep?"

I shook my head frantically and kept my hand on his chest only to push my body away.

"N-no. Forgive me, I-I can sit-"

"Sleep Ruby."

I had never been so close to a man before. This was so new to me. I was nervous every second. I have no clue what to do and King Xerxes wasn't holding back. Making it clear to me that he did not care about talks and people, I was officially his. Although I was worried if he could be gentle to me in bed. But I did not find his actions towards me offending.

His touch did not creep me, wasn't done completely against my will and I wondered if he just, knew I wouldn't dare refuse or I just didn't mind. That difference was something I ought to find

My sleep, I dare say became much more comfortable. He was warm, my head had a hard but softly enough man pillow. And before I knew it I was off to sleep. My mind woke up a while later. I heard slight chatter around.

We were passing through a village it seemed, As my senses came back, my body became highly aware of a hand on my lower back keeping me close to his chest. My head was lounging on his chest but one hand rested over his forearm and the other on my lap.

The carriage slowed and eventually came to a halt.

I heard King Xersex breathe in before moving. I was just so sleepy I didn't even care about moving my head. But I was aware of that big hand moving from my lower back to my waist and curling around me as the other opened the tiny window.

"A halt for the night sir. It is getting late."

‖ CHAPTER 9 ‖

" A halt for the night sir. It is getting late."

I heard Sir Andrew and finally opened my eyes to see a shawl over me.

"Understood" His musky voice replied.

I look down at my lap and I freeze. My bosom was practically hanging out. Well not hanging out. My laces had somehow come undone and my cleavage was out. Embarrassed I pushed myself up but he didn't let me move, I stayed still he tok off my shawl and tied my laces for me.

"Forgive me, I do not know how they-"

"I did."

That was all he said before he lifted me and sat me down on the seat before getting off and looking around then at me.

"Come," He said extending his hand and he waited as I adjusted my dress and hair. I did not wish to take any more time and grabbed his hand stepping down the carriage steps but forgot the shawl behind. Not a second later the footman closed the door and the carriage rode away to be washed off all the dirt and the horses to be fed.

The freezing wind suddenly slapped me and I shiver to hug myself.

I searched for Lydia but perhaps she was taken to the lodge to set the room up for me.

The King and Sir Andrew talked for a minute before King Xerxes took my hand, I stare with wide eyes as he did that with absolutely so hesitation or a second expression, to me it was like bees humming in my heart.

I look around and the village was under a thick fog but the nightlife was bustling. A heavy coat was put over my shoulders by the King as he continued walking. His hand grabbed mine again and I couldn't help but feel safe with him.

"We shall depart early. The mountains can be a challenge because of the carriage at night. It is best to halt here."

"I am aware. Write to Henry that we will be arriving tomorrow night and have the castle prepare for their Queen's arrival."

"Yes, most arrangements are made. Sir-"

We stopped at the garden which led to the dining area. King Xerxes let go of my hand and I pulled his coat closed to me and looked around while eves dropped on their conversations. Only stepping a few steps away to look at the flowers in the garden.

"We will have to arrange the ceremony the very next day. The Queen has to be -"

"Yes. I am aware. You do not need to tell me that Andrew."

I didn't look at him but, he seemed a bit angry. Every time his tone changed I felt frightened.

"Of course my King, however, I do show my concerns for the...ability to handle it. It would be wise to ask a Persia."

"Have her settle at court for the next week."

Sir Andrew nodded.

"The dinner is ready. I hope you have a good sleep." He said.

I walk to King Xerxes as he looked at me and gestured for me to take his hand. I shyly kept my hand over his and looked at Sir Andrew.

"Will you all not be joining us?"

"I-"

"It's alright we have some matters to discuss anyway. Come." The king said walking towards the dining table with me. Sir Andrew nodded with a small smile.

The dinner was heavenly. I had never tasted such a meal before. I enjoyed my food while they talked about things I had good knowledge about but had no interest in listening to. As I take the final sip of water and finished my meal I look out at the gardens.

Their conversations seemed serious enough that my presence seemed a bit too intruding.

"May I take a walk in the garden?" I asked.

"I shall call on your maid-"

"No, let them rest. I will be right here." I asked again which I told was something I shouldn't do since I had no idea how the King would react.

"Do not leave the garden." King Xerxes stated and I nodded walking out.

The air carried the scent of jasmine and mint from the bushes. It made me want to plant my own garden with vegetables and flowers. I used to love gardening until my mother started taking me back to court.

I wondered what she would be doing now. What Father is doing. I wondered how things work at the new court, and how the King's way of running his kingdom was. As a woman, I would not be involved in such matters.

I almost screamed as two hands wrapped around my waist, butterflies flew in my gut and my heart seem to have a field day beating so loud at the sudden touch every time. But I knew, at the back of my head. It was only he who could touch me.

"We have a long day ahead tomorrow. You have to sleep."

I nodded as he walked with me to my room. I thought it would be separate rooms until the doors opened revealing a large bed. Lydia had laid my nightgown on the chair at the vanity desk and I freeze.

In a bed, together, already?

I am not ready. I can't. I do not want to. Panic set in as King Xerxes locked the door and took off his clothes. He poured himself a drink and gulped down two sips.

No, no, no.

I am exhausted.

He looked at me and stared. For a while, "Well..? Do I have to command your to strip and get in bed?"

WHAT? strip? naked? already? But we aren't even back at the castle.

I was breathing heavily at this point. I wasn't ready. My heart dropped as he stood there looking out the window. Possibly waiting for me to get in bed and ...Oh goodness.

"I-I "

"What?" He asked. I flinched internally. All the things I found good about him had crashed down as he stares at me with a frustrated look.

"I am exhausted. F-Forgive me, My King." What was I doing? Refusing the King of his demands was a punishable offense. I could very well be forced into submission and no one would bat an eye.

My tears started forming as I see him walk towards me. I waited for some sort of harsh reaction but his hands cupped my face and pulled my face up to look at his.

His eyes are so dark... I thought.

"And what did you think I was going to do with you right now Ruby?"

I could not speak. I was afraid. So afraid.

"I-I am so sorry."

He closed his eyes letting go of my face. And gave a sigh of frustration.

"I am not asking you to open your legs so I can fuck you right now Ruby. I am asking you to strip, wear what your maid prepared, and go to sleep."

‖ CHAPTER 10 ‖

"I am not asking you to open your legs so I can fuck you right now Ruby. I am asking you to strip, wear what your maid prepared, and go to sleep."

Oh..

"I-Oh."

He turns around and takes another sip of that liquor.

"Go to bed Ruby, now." My body always obeyed his command even before my eyes could register.

I sniff once before walking to the power room beside the bedroom, not before grabbing my nightwear. Lydia had prepared a hot bath for me. I took a short bath and brushed my hair before wearing that nightgown. When I looked at myself in the mirror my stomach twisted.

"Why Lydia? You little brat-"

That was quite a revealing nightgown. My breasts weren't as visible but clearly out there. I assume she did it because she thought the same as me. I was utterly embarrassed. The dress had long sleeves but it was quite frankly a bit see-through. However much I did not wish to wear it, it was this or my morning petticoat whose hem was covered in mud.

I wrapped myself in the shawl kept near the bath and walked out. The candles had been blown out except for the ones beside the bed. King Xerxes was nowhere to be seen. Perhaps he was out. I quickly got in bed as the cold air did not allow me to stay out and snuggled in the warm bedsheet.

It was after a while that I heard the door open and closed. I heard the locks and soon the space beside me dipped. I felt the freezing cold air sneak in as the bedsheet was lifted and he lay there with my back to him.

Even if he was far, I could feel his warmth. I felt like I could feel his hands on me.

It was the silence that frustrate me. I wondered if I would ever have an honest normal conversation with him. A friend and husband before my King.

I was asking for too much.

I suck in a deep breath as he moved and curled his hand around my waist pulling me into him. He was so warm. His bare chest touched my back it was like burning coal. I gulp fussing in my head.

I was in bed! with a stranger! A man at that.

"Calm down, You are shivering." He whispered and I realized I was shivering this whole time. Perhaps these people were so used to the weather they didn't care.

"S-sorry."

"I do not like you apologizing for such menial things Ruby."

"Sorry-"

I realized my mistake but my fussy self kept repeating my mistake, "Oh. Sorry-"

" Shut up." He groans pulling me closer. He nuzzled his face in my neck and I almost moan at that feeling.

His hand stayed right under my breasts, his other hand under my head. His torso was pressed against my back and I had no way out of this feeling. I felt myself getting tingles down there. I had no understanding of these feelings I could only stay quiet and love it.

"Madam.." Lydia's voice run in my ears and I turned around hugging the blanket closer as the cold air touched my skin.

"Madam it is morning, you will be late for breakfast."

I opened my eyes and stayed there for a moment until I realized where I was. Not my room that's for sure. Last night's events run through my mind and blush.

"Careful Ma'am." Lydia helped me out of the bath and wrapped my body in the cotton cloth.

"I hope you packed a comfortable dress for me, Lydia, If I have to sit for hours I'd do it in a simple dress."

She nodded smiling.

"Forgive me for not packing an extra coat on hand, I had your white coat taken out of the luggage. I was told this morning the mountains are expecting snow."

"Snow?! But its still autumn"

"Oh well, we are going across the tallest mountains, It starts snowing in the middle of August usually."

I sigh wearing my petticoat and turning around so she could lace it up. She gave me my sage green dress and laced it up from the back and did my hair finishing it off with a white ribbon in my hair.

"Uh-Madam, do I need to take the sheets off?"

She looked at me like I did something. I blush staring at her and slowly shook my head.

"N-No! nothing happens!"

She held back her laughter and nodded, bowing one before leaving me be.

I look at the bed and wonder when King Xerxes woke up. Last night he held me so tight I swear I have never felt so...so different before. The sort of tingling I got in me, I felt like my body had butterflies hopping around.

I make my way down the stairs to the dining room with Lydia behind me. She leads me to a balcony on the first floor reserved for us. The guards opened the door and I see King Xerxes with his back to us talking with Sir Andrew. He snapped at me and he looked back with a natural look.

"This way Your Highness." said one of the maids and I smiled sitting down at the table and looking out at the scenic view

I have some tea looking at the two exceptionally large men. In fact, all of the soldiers were easily towering over us, humans. But King Xerxes and Sir Andrew had something about them that induced a natural fear in all. Perhaps the fact that they were werewolves.

"Eat well, it will be cold as we travel up the mountain." I nodded as King Xerxes sat next to me before saying that.

I wanted to have a conversation. Maybe ask him if he has breakfast or what he liked but I couldn't quite bring myself to do so. I felt as if talking to him in public might ruin his reputation of being a serious man.

"More tea ma'am?" Lydia asked and I nodded. She looked at the servant. One of them, a young man walked towards us and gave me a new cup pouring me more tea. The wind suddenly blew across the balcony shaking the table wear and the boy himself as he stumbled with his hands and the tea fell on my hand. I whip my hand away at the sudden burn causing the man to gasp and set the pot down bowing.

"Forgive me, your highness. Forgive me, Alpha King, I-I didn't-"

"It's alright-" My voice was greatly overshadowed by King Xerxes.

"Get out!"

I flinch as he grabbed my hand watching the poor man walk away and I frown. The young man bowed and stumbled to get back up before walking away in fear. My eyes stare at King Xerxes in sadness as the king dipped his kerchief in water and rest it over my hand.

I couldn't speak when he was angry. I only look at the boy as he disappeared into the hall.

"Shall we change the teacup, I apologize-"

"It's quite alright, I will take it to form here thankyou." Sir Andrew stepped in as the owner tried to make it better.

Sir Andrew gestured if I wanted another tea and smiled stopping him before taking the Teapot myself and pouring the tea into a new cup. I ate some light breakfast before we departed.

‖ CHAPTER 11 ‖

I waited for Lydia as she brought me a small bag of necessary items I might need for the travel for she cannot get off the carriage and help me on the narrow roads.

"Napkins, medicine, water, bread and some scent for if you may get sick due to the travel. And your mother told me you maybe be expecting your bleeding so I am carrying another dress with me. Let me know when we halt."

I smiled nodding as she gave the coat and bag to the footman who kept it under the seat.

King Xerxes was waiting for me by the door. I bite my lip as I took his hand and got in while he followed me, I just didn't expect him to sit beside me again. I take the shawl keeping it on my lap feeling nervous around him.

The mountains were a sight to be seen. It was so beautiful covered in snow I wondered how the soldiers managed to ride their horses in such chilly weather. I was worried one would catch a cold. As we ascended the mountain the carriage got colder and I saw the soldiers put on heavy coats.

"Ruby" I look back to King Xerxes from the view who had opened his long dark fur coat and gestured me to get close. I blushed feeling butterflies in my stomach and scared to do so but gave in, scooting closer than I already was so he could drape his coat over my shoulder and pull me into his warm body. He was really warm. How could their body be so hot?

I lay my head on his shoulder and fussed about their body heat while the carriage made its way toward the top of the mountains. Before long we stopped for a bathroom break at one of the last lodges on the mountains.

As I take the King's hand my eyes fell on the breathtaking view. The valley under and the trees covered with snow but a bright clear sky with the warm sun made me sit here forever and eat all I want and sleep in the snow itself.

As I stepped out, King Xerxes wrapped his hand around my waist and walked me towards the lodge.

"Don't take long." He whispered in my ear sending goosebumps down my body. I bite my lips and nodded before walking with Lydia and one of the guards.

She helped me freshen up and fix my dress before I walk out.

"Sir Russel will guide you back to His Majesty for tea, I'll be back "

I frown giving and sigh, "Lydia! we have been sisters before friends since my childhood, of course, I will wait for you while you do your business."

Lydia pouts smiling softly before going into the powder room.

"I hope you find the country to your liking Madam." I turn to the young soldier and smile.

"Yes, it is beautiful," I answered. My eyes followed King Xerxes and Sir Andrew as they discussed a matter few feet away while I had tea.

"You will love our kingdom as well, the forests are especially breathtaking."

I smile listing to him talk as one other soldier walked towards us and talk about their villages. I laugh at their light-hearted jokes.

"Well, yes our village has had one of the strongest warriors so far. They were all born under the Beta's family tree."

I look at the young man whose name was Mark as he introduced it.

"What is Beta?"

They stopped their chatters and looked at me.

"You do not know what a Beta is? well, it is the Second and only command under the Alpha."

I frown.

"Alpha-"

"Madam have you never read books in your life-" They laughed softly as I smile in confusion.

Before we knew it their laughter was cut off as the tip of a sword stopped inches away from his mouth. His eyes trembled right before the sword and he fell to his knees with his head bowed.

"I have spoken out of line My king, Please show me mercy"

I stare at the man unable to understand why his life was suddenly hanging on his plea for mercy. I shift my eyes slowly, up to the owner of the sword, King Xerxes. Who stood with his eyes in a menacing gaze looking down at the two soldiers.

"You dare question your queen's literacy?" Sir Andrew asked.

I gasp slightly as King Xerxes pressed the tip of the sword into Mark's chest drawing blood. I stood up in worry but couldn't move. I couldn't say anything.

My literacy? It was just a light-hearted question for amusement. How was that offending?

I look back at the soldiers and then at King Xerxes.

"Back to your posts," King commands them and they scrambled to stand up and leave.

I watch as King Xerxes retracts his sword back into his scabbard and looked at me. I look down having no courage to question his actions. But my fear raises as I see everyone leaving us be. I whimper as his fingers curl below my chin and raised my head to meet his gaze.

I stared into his deep void-like eyes as he observed something about me.

"You are frightened." He stated.

Well yes of course I would be, after such an act.

"I-I-" I stumble upon my words but unfortunately his eyes were just too intimidating for me to speak or comprehend my own words.

"I spare his life for your eyes. He would be long dead now Ruby. Be acclimated to such situations now for I suspect it might happen often."

I stare out the window as the view passed by, my mind jumping back and forth at the King's mood. One moment he is peaceful and the other filled with anger. I fear I might have annoyed him in some way or another.

I felt my heart stop as he played with my hair, his fingers kept curling my hair around and I was getting hot second by second.

I wanted him to stop but I just never felt this way before. I wasn't pleased my curly hair was played with, however, he... I liked it somehow. It was a subtle way of showing me attention and I found it most alluring.

It didn't take long till I was suddenly scooped up in his arms and placed between his legs with my head over his chest as he leaned back. I could hear his heart, with all the light armor The king wore, I could still stay warm and hear his heart like he was wearing nothing.

Being this close to him made me feel as if I was on the edge of a cliff. In fear of falling but curious if I did fall, what would happen to me?

"If you need to halt, let me know."

I was in shock at his tone. It changed with every man he talked with. With Sir Andrew, it was stern but patient. With soldiers it sounded scary, and with me...I found it calm but with his causal stern statements. I found myself nodding and obeying without any second thoughts.

We halted for a few minutes to have tea. I didn't wish to leave the carriage so I shook my head at Lydia who asked me if I needed her.

I move to let The King go but he held me back. My face flushed hard as He held me close while Sir Andrew walked towards the window and talked. I was so embarrassed I hid my face in his chest.

"Any casualties ?"

The king asked as he slowly took my palm in his hand and rubbed his thumb over the back of my hand. I stare at his rough hand over mine and blocked everything around us.

An overwhelming urge to look at him, his eyes, and feel his lips under my fingertips passed over me. I see the King dropping the curtains over the windows as Sir Andrew walked away. My head suddenly started spinning as I thought of his lips. My neck felt hotter suddenly as I breathed in slowly. my chest raises and falls slowly as I feel the pressure of his eyes on me.

It felt like I was pressed between two walls, I couldn't move. I let my curious mind get the better of me and look up at him. Into the Lycan King's eyes. Something no one dares to do. Something people were killed for as it showed challenging the king's power.

Black. Pure black with a grey ring along his iris. His eyes were like a sudden hit. It was his nature, not as a human but something beyond it that made his normal pretty eyes absolutely terrifying, I held my breath as he looked at me. His hand had grabbed mine in a tight hold now.

I ignored my fear because my other hand moved on its own and placed my index finger over his light pink lips. They were so soft.

I felt everything turn quiet and dark as all I could see were his eyes and feel his lower lip under my finger. My body was pressed against his, I heard him breathing softly, his eyebrows were sharp so was his jaw.

The silence between us was like the gently calm sea with darkness surrounding it.

My finger slipped across his lip and before I could understand his hand curled around my neck from behind and pulled me in. My mouth left a half gasp as his lips crashed on mine.

I felt like fireworks burst inside my heart.

|| CHAPTER 12 ||

[Xerxes Lycan]

I push the curtains back of the window and see the maid looking at my wife. The maid tried her best to not tremble under my gaze as she softly asked Ruby if she needed her assistance, Ruby shook her head and looked down.

I could tell how sleepy she was. Perhaps she was too nervous to sleep. I did not understand why she would be so nervous and scared around me. Irrespective of her nature as a human, she would feel the mate bond. I wondered if she was just far too worried about her life with me.

I see Andrew get off his horse and walk towards our carriage. I grabbed Ruby's hand to feel if she was cold. As I suspected, her hands were cold as ice. I rubbed my thumb over her hand to warm it up as Andrew bowed. She moved her head into my chest, shy as she was making me clench my jaw in dire need of grabbing her and just never letting go.

Just the thought of a man seeing my mate gave me anxiety, anger, and the need to pull their eyes off. Even Andrew.

"Any Casualties?"

He nodded with a worried look, " We found multiple bodies. In human form, the bites suggest a fight, we suspect it was a rouge Wolf. He must've tried to get them to submit."

I raised my head staring at Andrew and thinking.

"Have someone look into this when we get back."

Andrew nodded as I dropped the curtain having no desire to show my comfortable mate to any soldier out there.

My heart constantly itching to claim her right here and fuck her was overwhelming. But she wasn't just anyone, she was my queen, Part of my love for her was respecting her. But the lord did not give me enough strength to hold myself back like so. I felt angry every time I looked at her knowing she wasn't yet claimed by me and knowing very well how badly my wolf wanted her in my arms tight.

The silence between us wasn't bad, she was in my arms. Letting me touch her. That was enough..for now. But I wouldn't be surprised if I just claimed her right now as she had her head over my chest listing to my heart. I felt vulnerable letting her listen to my heart.

I felt as if she could control me right here.

I see her breath heavy as I held her hand tight and suddenly she looked up catching me off guard I stare at pure little eyes as she stared into mine. Her chest was pressed over mine and I wanted to rip this amour off me to just feel a little of her skin over mine.

I chuckle in my head a little at the daring move she made. I knew the effect I had on humans, my own kind couldn't look me in my eyes as I was sending them their dead warning right there. I had that control over them but she tried. And I was proud she did.

I was so immersed in her eyes I didn't see her finger coming near me. I felt my heart stop as she kept her finger over my lower lip lightly, A feather touch. Exactly as I expected from her. So soft, fragile, and like touch like a feather.

Even her fingertips carried a soft scent.

I was lost in her eyes while my hands curl around her waist slowly holding her toward and trapping her little body between my chest and my arms.

And when she brushed her finger across my lower lip I lost her. Grabbing her neck from being and kissing her beautiful soft sweet lips. I couldn't hold back as I kissed her dangerously rough. She gasped but she could only make half of it. She whimpered lightly putting her fist right under my collar and lightly pushing back but I just couldn't stop.

She couldn't keep up as I kissed her upper lip and then her plump lower lip. Licking her lips as I kissed her over and over again while one hand had her held against me and the other moved her cup her cheek tightly while her little arms held a fist over my chest.

In the end, she whimpered as slowly kissed me back. I pushed myself back with much contemplation to let her breathe and not scare her. She was breathing heavily, with her fists still over my chest and her head dropped down and I see her chest heaving slowly. She blinked unable to move as I held her to me while I stare at her.

I kissed her cheek once before tucking her hair behind her ear. I felt something burst in my heart as I see her. She was red as a tomato. Her cheeks, nose, lips, and chest it was all a shade of red and she was warm as she could be.

Her lips were shining because of me. I felt the need to curse every man who had seen my mate's beautiful lips and her cleavage. I sigh leaning back and pulling her fall on me. She did not resist falling on my chest and now breathing slowly.

"I will not hold myself back anymore Ruby. I am not like those who will wait, I am a cruel man with cruel desires and you are one of them." I whispered as she looked up at me.

Her hands were still on my chest and her eyes now twinkling, I could see her fear but I could see how she willingly submitted to me.

She looked back down but I clenched my jaw in anger grabbing her chin and pulling her head up to look at me.

"You are under no obligation to submit to me as my Queen but I will not tolerate disobeying me as your husband. Do you understand me?"

She stared at me for a moment before nodding slowly and I felt like I had scared her.

"Will you obey me ?" I asked and she gulped trembling.

Fuck..I scared her.

She nodded but I cupped her cheeks and kissed her lips before pulling away.

"You do not have to. But you are mine. " I said before kissing her deeply again.

She moaned into the kiss giving me pure bliss as she tried her best to keep up with me. I felt my heart sore as she fist my coat in her hand and raised her head to kiss me better. I let go as I see the tail tale signs of my cock harden and sigh. Any more and I will have her bend over here in this carriage right now.

I stare at her little face as she lay on my chest and soon closed her eyes with her tight hold on my forearm. I looked away unable to stop my boner any longer.

We reached the borders of my kingdom soon enough after crossing the mountains but Had to hault for refreshments.

Ruby rubbed her eyes as she woke up making me stare her at all over again. She blushed the minute she saw herself hugging me in her sleep and let go. I lift her up and set her on the seat before adjusting my attired and looking at her.

Fuck me..

She looked so arousing. Her bust was purely visible as she had taken her cost off a while ago. The dress did a go job of hugging her curves and breasts. I take my coat off and hand it to her.

"Wear this," I said opening the carriage and getting out.

The cold wind passed by and I realized how hot the carriage was. My soldiers bowed to me before taking their horses to be fed.

I look at Andrew as he walked towards me and looked at the carriage realizing his Queen wasn;t out.

"Fetch the maid-"

"Yes I did Sir. SHe will be here soon. Do I need to call any physician if her highness needs it?"

I looked back at the carriage and think before walking to it again and opening the door to see my mate adjusting her gown.

There was nothing I could do but watch her shriek silently and stop herself as I stood there with a sudden hard cock. I thanked my attire which made it impossible for people to see it.

"Just me," I whispered as I cupped her cheek and brushed my thumb over her cheek before letting go.

I smirk in my head as I see her relax.

"Do I need to call a physician? Do you feel good?"

"Y-Yes your Majesty, I am fine."

Probably the first few words she spoke to me for the past four hours. I nodded waiting as she adjusted her dress and I give her my hand to get down.

She shivered to get down the carriage and looking around her her maid came to her aid. I stare at the maid she grabbed her hand and guides her inside the tent put up for her.

"Any orders?" Andrew must have noticed my eyes over that maid.

I nodded, "Keep an eye on her."

Andrew nodded.

"I want a woman with good combat skills as one of the ladies in waiting," I order.

"I will have that arranged."

I watch Ruby walk out the tend with gloves over hand and talking with that maid. Her hair flowed in the chilly wind and her cheeks were flushed red.

"Andrew-"

"Yes, your majesty?" He asked as I see my mate walk towards us.

"No one is allowed to request the presence of the Queen unless My or your approval is given, it applies to the royal family as well."

"Of course." He answered.

‖ CHAPTER 13 ‖

As I look at King Xerxes my stomach flips remembering what we did back in the carriage and walking back in the same carriage made me even more nervous to say anything.

I was frozen, couldn't speak, and was utterly shocked as he grabbed me and kissed me. I didn't even know it was allowed to kiss the king. Oh... I was married to him, I forgot who I was.

I gulp sipping on the cup of tea and watching the road ahead.

"Madam." Lydia hands me my kerchief and I thank her for wiping my runny nose. Every since I got out my nose was runny.

I finish my tea quite quickly and set it down on the table ahead. Within a minute one of the local men who prepared the tea came to clean the table for us. He bowed to me and I smiled back at him.

"Shall we get going your Highness?" Sir Andrew asked and I nodded getting up and walking toward the carriage with King Xerxes leading the way and Sir Andrew behind me while the soldiers got on their horses.

"Uh- Y-Your H-highness!"

I stopped turning around at the same man running toward us. Not a moment after I blink the king had walked before me blocking my view from that man while Sir Andrew walked to stand to my other side.

I watched in worry as the man, now scared of their reaction to his call, slowly bowed his hand presenting my handkerchief in his hand and extending it.

"Oh-"

I didn't realize I had dropped it. King Xerxes slowly lowered his guard and watched that man but I stepped forward to thank him. Unfortunately, I was suddenly pushed back by my waist. Ignoring the butterflies in my tummy and I look at Sir Andrew who took the kerchief from that man's hand and handed him extra coins as a gesture of thanks.

I smiled at that man who did not dare lift his gaze from his bow.

"Ruby."

I nodded walking back to the carriage and sitting down. I looked out towards Sir Andrew who held my kerchief but before I asked for it he threw it into a fire burning nearby. I frown as King Xerxes sits down beside me. As if he knew exactly what I was staring at he looked at the fire before me and closed the door.

"We cannot risk you getting infected by their touch. Even a cloth can be a risk."

"B-but they didn't seem ill-"

"The mountains carry a lot of illness in people because of the cold. Believe me, Andrew did it for the better."

I nodded leaning back on the seat.

As the carriage entered the kingdom borders I look outside at the secluded road leading towards the castle, the back road to avoid the villages and large towns. I feel my heart getting heavy as I take a deep breath and think how different it would be.

The carriage stopped and I gulp as the footman opened the door. King Xerxes was the first to step out and he nodded at someone who stood out in my vision. I licked my lips scooting towards the door and I wait for King Xerxes to help me down as he had done before. But He didn't. I watched new women walk up to me, her attire clearly different than anyone around, bold and scary. She stopped before the door and bowed before she extended her hand I look at it before glancing at the King who never looked back at me.

With a sudden heart ace, I take her and let her help me down. As my eyes looked up, I took in the huge walls of the border standing strong before the castle behind it. I stare in complete awe at the black stoned border covered in beautiful vines and lush trees possible to cover the road leading up to the hidden back gate.

"This way your highness." said the woman who had helped me.

I look down at her and then at the King who has taken his steps ahead of me towards the gate. I frown unable to understand his sudden coldness.

Had I angered him?

I walked slowly towards the gates having no desire to embarrass the King by standing beside him.

I smile at the butler standing before the gate who bowed at me before leading us in.

"Any new reports?" King Xerxes asked and he disappeared into a different hall I was left standing there with no explanation. Only for a few moments before the women came back again.

"I will be your guard as appointed by Sir Andrew. My name is Clara. I am at your disposal."

I wanted to stop them from bowing every time they talked but I didn't know how to.

"It is good to meet you, Clara. Thank you for guarding me."

"This way-" She said stepping aside and gesturing me towards the stairs leading somewhere.

"This is the back of the castle. This is where your chambers will be." She mentioned as we walked through the empty corridors.

As soon we entered the chamber I blink and stare at the huge room. To my left laid gowns over a large couch and multiple wardrobes and vanity and to my right the bed with two different rooms to either side of the bed.

"I will be sleeping with your personal lady in waiting in the chamber connecting to yours my Queen," Clara said walking to the right door of the bed and I followed her. It was another powder room where I could get ready and have tea with large windows. I watched in utter shock as she opened a concealed door that led to a large room.

"This goes on forever," I whispered and turned around only to be stopped as three women stood before me.

"Good evening Madam. I will be your secondary maid Maya. I shall take care of your dressing and bath. Mia and April will be looking after trivial matters. Please let us know if you need anything. We shall ask your personal Lady for your likes and dislikes."

I smiled nodding and look at Lydia who gulped at the overwhelming pressure.

"Thank you," I whispered before walking back into the main chamber.

"Will the King be sleeping in a different-"

"Yes, as he wished. The main chambers for You my Queen and King are through there." She said pointing at the door beside the fireplace in front for my bed.

"This side of the corridor will be your personal chambers. I shall give you a tour once you have recovered from your journey."

I nodded sitting on the bed.

"We have already prepared a bath and all necessary things for your grooming madam. Please this way"

I walked into my bathroom as I sigh at the luxurious parlor. This was what I got in turn for my happiness and possible sadness. With the way, King Xerxes acted the minute we got back it was possible he did not wish to show any concern for me in his kingdom. After all, I was just a human.

I let them take off my clothes and undo my hair. I stopped Maya before she took my petticoat off.

"Uh-I-"

"I will let Miss Lydia handle the rest"

I sigh in happiness that she understood. I wasn't comfortable letting women see me except Lydia. I was just shy.

|| CHAPTER 14 ||

"It will be your first appearance before the court as our Queen tomorrow your highness. I hope you rest well." Maya stated as she brushed my hair while Lydia helped me put up my stockings.

I stare into the mirror at myself. Wondering why King Xerxes acted so warmly before reaching his castle and suddenly his behaviour turned cold.

Was it I who failed to assume proper etiquette or was it something out of my mind's reach?

My hair was half tied up with a white ribbon and lace nightwear. It was so soft and comfortable. As Lydia said, none of the property I owned before was taken into this kingdom I was to come empty-handed with only two people who were for my service, I even the gown I dressed in was never given back to me. I was to wear the jewels and clothes given only by my current kingdom. Many of the things we took were just our precious items. Even those were questioned before keeping them in my chambers.

The dresses I wore on the travel except my wedding gown were thrown away.

"Would it be possible to disturb Your Highness for a quick fit?"

I snapped my head back to an old pretty lady with two women behind her. I look at Maya as she looked at me.

"They are your seamstresses, your highness-"

"Just -" I cut her off unable to stand the constant title they added with every sentence, "-call me Madam. Please."

Maya nodded and I nod at the seamstress giving them permission to enter.

"Forgive us Madam but we did get measurements from your old corset, but I wanted to be sure that your gowns are of proper fit." Said the old lady as she slowly took off my nightwear revealing my thin nightgown.

"It's all right, if you need to ask any questions about my likes and dislikes you can ask Lydia," I said gesturing towards her. She smiled as the seamstress nodded.

"Does your highness prefer linen or cotton for your nightgowns?"

I blink at her and got stuck on the sudden question as I never care for such trivial details.

"I don't mind either..? I suppose?" I answered with an uncertain gaze to Lydia who held back her laugh.

"Madam would like linen better for sleeping." She stated and they nodded continuing on the measurements.

They left soon after and I watch them bow before closing the door as I put on my robe and pin it.

I was uncertain what would happen from tomorrow, this beautiful chamber given to me seemed like the only safe haven for me now. I sit near the fireplace warming myself and staring at the floor.

"Would you like some warm milk, Madam?" Maya asked putting a knitted blanket over me. I smiled pulling it to my chest and nodded.

"She understands you well. I am surprised." Lydia said sitting on the small table beside me and looking at the fire.

I sigh sleeping on the couch on my side and nodding.

"They were prepared for that I suppose?" I asked and she shrugged.

"Why do I need so many ladies around me I do not understand." I groan closing my eyes and fidgeting with the blanket.

"Because you are the Queen. I suppose I have to look after bigger things than just your hair and gowns now."

I chuckled in sadness.

"Oh, did you see Sir Fred?"

Lydia nodded, "He asked me to give his apologies for not receiving us at the gates. He seemed quite occupied with handling some court affairs."

It must be about the treaty then. I hope he is okay.

"You can go now, Lydia. You are tired as well."

She stood up bowing before leaving me be. I let the sound of the burning wood engulf my mind as I enjoyed the warmth.

"Madam." I snap my head at Maya who sets a glass of milk on the table beside me.

"You may go now, Thank you."

She smiled bowing as well before leaving me alone.

The warm milk helped me get sleepy, I didn't feel like setting my foot on the floor as I snuggled up on the couch and let the sleep take over me. Not a moment later I heard the door beside my bed open and close.

Before I could think if it was Lydia or Maya my eyes snapped open at the sudden touch. I was scooped up in his arms and before I could comprehend he was walking towards the bed. I stayed quite in shock as he puts me on the bed and walks back before stripping himself.

While I sat up on the bed watching him in all his glory. His body was large, his torso defined and I could see scars all over his chest and arms.

His arms...why were they so huge?

I gasp as he pushed me to lie down with his hand over my chest. I felt my body highly responsive to every touch he gave me. I stared at his hand unhooking my robe and revealing my thin gown. My nipples now exposed to the cold air suddenly perked up. But the loose nightgown thankfully didn't make them obvious.

I gulp unable to work my mind as I give in to him. His lips laid on my neck and my shoulder pulled in at the sudden tingles I got. He didn't talk but his hands brushed over my waist before falling to my legs and pulling up my dress.

I was nervous, embarrassed as I had no knowledge of how this went.

I gasp as his lips touched my collar. My mind was now in a haze as I closed my eyes and let my body engulf his warmth and kisses. I whimpered as he bites my neck before my hands rest over his shoulders.I could only moan as he pushed my legs aside riping away the hooks of my nightdress and exposing my bare chest.

He pushed away and laid still as his eyes travelled from my face to my neck, his thumb brushed back and forth on a spot of my neck below my ear before his eyes and fingers moved down to my collarbone and then my bare breasts.

"Fuck"

I heard him grunt under his breath as he dove in kissing my neck and biting me making me whimper and squirm under his arms. I gasp again as he touched my breasts and squeezed them. I held back my moan as he went harsher on them.

"Ah! That-that hurts.." My last words were a mere whisper as he continued fondling them.

His fingers suddenly pinched my nipple and I let out a soft cry at the highly sensitive part of my body. Too bad I didn't know how sensitive my nether reigns could be with him near them. As I found myself moaning and blushing red as his hand softly cupped me down there and rubbed his finger over me.

"N-No. That's, that's too much" I whispered covering my face but he held my hand beside my face and kissed me.

His kisses were rough, he pulled and bit my lower lip, licked my lips, and had his tongue collided with mine. And all I could do was tremble and follow his kiss when he pushed apart my legs and laid between them, a fear settled in the pit of my stomach.

And when I felt it, for the first time. I was scared to my death.

That possibly couldn't fit inside me. Lydia had told me all the birds and bee talk but this was just impossible. I stare at his ..manhood in fear of how badly it would hurt. When his finger slowly circled around me. I threw my head back embarrassed and scared but didn't resist. After all, I could never deny the King. I had to give him an heir. Or I would never be respected in this court.

My eyes filled with tears as I suddenly thought of that. I didn't want the burden of birthing a child so young at my age. I wanted to wait. I wanted to do so many things before this.

I closed my eyes as he pushed his finger inside me and I cry out in pain. My tears now fall down my cheek as he pushed in and out. The sudden pleasure from his action was a shock as my eyes shed tears but I liked it.

I hated that I liked it. Not because of him, but because of the harsh pressure I would face as I would walk out. I would be constantly asked about my duties. I did not want to be bed bound so soon.

He pulled out his finger and I whimper out loud as he tried to push himself inside me.

But as I anticipate that dreadful pain he had suddenly stopped. My eyes stayed closed for a few moments before I open them there was his hand on my waist and the other on my cheek. I dare not look into his eyes but he pushed my chin up to look at him.

"I won't -" He whispered before a kiss landed on my lips and he leans back sitting on the bed.

What had I done?

Dread set inside my heart as I stare at his back in fear. The first dread, was because he had rejected me. I had displeased the king and now my future was only in the dungeons. And the second, was when my eyes laid upon his bare back. The scars.

He stood up walking two steps ahead and I feel as if he would dispose of me that very moment.

"F-Forgive me." I blurt out, my tears now slipping down my neck as I sat up my hands slowly pulling my nightdress to cover my chest. He stopped and looked back at me. I saw his eyes go wide as I look down and stand up.

"I-I was -I don't how to. But I can take it-"

"Ruby."

I heard his voice in my ears. I wondered how fast he got right in front of me.

I sniff as he picked me up in his arms and I gasp circling my hand around his neck, my head down in fear.

He sat on the couch before the mantle and settled me over his lap. I could feel my stomach twist and turn with arousal and embarrassment.

"I am sorry," I said with a sniff.

He cupped my chin and pushed me to face him. There was a moment of silence between us as he kissed my cheek.

"I shall not until you are ready."

"I am ready. I assure you. Your Majesty, I only wish to give you an heir as soon as possible. That..is my only duty" I whispered.

His demeanour changed so quickly, As he clenched his jaw and looked away. I frown trying to understand what has suddenly angered him.

"You think I only want an heir? You think I married you so you could just sit here and give me a child?" He grunts and I gulp.

He suddenly sets me down on the couch and stands up looking away while his hands brushed across his hair.

"I-I was told it would make you and the court happy-" I stopped myself. I had no idea what could anger him even more.

He snapped his head at me and I look up at him in fear.

"I-I forgive me-"

"Ruby." His voice was so addicting.

"I am disappointed in what you think of me."

I gasp in my head.

"No! No...your majesty-"

"IT Is Xerxes for you !" I flinch, although he didn't scream he spoke clearly and sternly but now I cloud tell why everyone feared him. There was a heavy weight to his voice, something no one could do. His voice sends shivers down my spine.

"I-I do not know what would offend you and what wouldn't," I said so softly.

I cover my mouth in shock as he kneels before me and grabbed my neck pulling me closer.

"You are my Queen. So Act like it. I do not wish to do anything unless you are ready."

I frown and shook my head.

"So you-you aren't angry?" I questioned and he sighs pulling me to stand up and lifting me up. I let my arms cling to his neck as my legs wrapped around his torso. My heart filled with flutters as he sat on the couch with me on him. I let go of his neck and let my arms rest on his extremely huge biceps.

"No Lycan can hurt his mate. One should die if he does."

"But I am not-" I stopped myself as I feel tingles and butterflies in my stomach. I suddenly looked into his eyes for some reason and just stare at them. I felt like he was saying something through them. Had I not thought about it, I would've never known. As the thoughts of Lycans having mates dwelled upon me, I gasp.

"I can't be.." I whispered but he kissed me deeply.

"I couldn't believe it either-" He said grabbing my waist tighter and wrapping his hand around my neck as we kissed.

"But I am a human-" I said between the kisses and he hummed kissing me roughly. I pulled away breathing heavily and put the back of my hand on my lips.

"You are mine. Mine for eternity."

CHAPTER 15

I gasp in my head.

"No! No...your majesty-"

"IT Is Xerxes for you !" I flinch, although he didn't scream. His voice sends shivers down my spine.

"I-I do not know what would offend you and what wouldn't," I said so softly.

I cover my mouth in shock as he kneels before me and grabbed my neck pulling me closer.

"You are my Queen. So Act like it. I do not wish to do anything unless you are ready."

I frown and shook my head.

"So you-you aren't angry?" I questioned and he sighs pulling me to stand up and lifting me up. I let my arms cling to his neck as my legs wrapped around his torso. My heart filled with flutters as he sat on the couch with me on him. I let go of his neck and let my arms rest on his extremely huge arms.

"No Lycan can hurt his mate. One should die if he does."

"But I am not-" I stopped myself as I feel tingles and butterflies in my stomach. I suddenly looked into his eyes for some reason and just stare at them.

"I can't be.." I whispered but he kissed me deeply.

"I can't believe it either-" He said grabbing my waist and my wrapping his hand around my neck as we kissed.

"But I am a human-" I said between the kisses and he hummed kissing me roughly. I pulled away breathing heavily and put the back of my hand on my lips.

"You are mine. Mine for eternity."

He didn't consummate that night. He said he would wait and have me to his fullest when I was ready than claim me now and leave me hurt. Although I wished to say I wanted it, I said nothing.

I wasn't prepared for the Lycan king to act in such a way. It was new, unexpected considering the cruel actions he had done. Was it truly how he felt or was this an act? It would break my heart if it was.

We slept that night in peace. His hands wrapped around my waist as his chest pressed against my back. He didn't let go till morning.

It was surreal, the King wanted to wait until I was comfortable, that was the most respect I was given as a lady.

I woke up feeling fuzzy, my body hurt because of the long travel. I lay there staring at the ceiling till I felt a heavy hand over my stomach. I panic seeing the King sleeping soundly beside me. He was so huge, like a bear beside me. I gulped trying to move but to my shock, he pulled me closer.

I had forgotten how he stripped me naked last night and hugged me under the woollen blanket. I was naked as a wee baby. His length now suddenly poking my waist and his hand right below my breasts made me wet between my legs.

I blush as he nuzzled his face in my neck. The tickling didn't stop on my neck and he breathed in deeply before moving to sleep over my chest. I stayed still contemplating a lot before my eyes landed on his hair.

They looked so smooth. My fingers ran across his head enjoying his soft fluffy hair under my fingers forgetting who he was for a moment.

"How long have you been awake." He asked snapping me out of my little bubble and I move my hand away just an inch only for his hand to grab mine.

He looked up at me through his thick lashes. His eyes were so sharp they could cut through lies.

"N-not long," I said softly.

He hummed falling back on my chest, My eyes go wide as his hand softly caressed my right breast while his lips laid light kisses over my neck.

I moan unable to hold it any longer and he grunts.

"I hope you forgive me for what I might do tonight."

I look at him as he wraps his hand around my waist before running his hands up and down my torso giving me butterflies.

"I-I do not mind doing it," I whispered. But his sudden chuckle grabbed my attention.

"I am not talking about fucking Ruby"

The amount of sudden heat that creeps into my chest and neck as he said that was unbearable. I could feel my cheeks get hot as he stared at me. But I ignored the butterflies and asked for his answer.

"Th-then?" I asked. He grabbed my hand pulling it to rest over his head. I continued my play with his soft hair as he demanded me to with his eyes.

"I wish to mark you as mine."

It felt as if he had engulfed the body of my soul completely, His skin touching mine was too unbearable as the constant sparks kept bursting in my body but it was too much.

"I thought I was yours the moment I married you, my king."

That slipped from my tongue quite easily, I gasp as he wrapped his fingers around my neck and squeezed it. My mind was rather on his length, hard on my lower belly. His long hand extended from his fingers around my neck, his wrist down to between my breasts and his elbow below them. It felt different, arousing if I could comprehend.

"What did I ask you to call me when we are alone Ruby?"

His husky voice now demanded an answer in such a tone that I was obligated to give me a reply.

"Xerxes" I whispered and he lets go of my neck cupping my cheek, brushing his thumb softly over it before his hand went down to my breasts and cupped them.

I closed my eyes as his lips touched my chest, going to my nipples and he suddenly bites me making me shriek.

"Forgive me, I cannot hold my wolf back any longer."

And with that, I felt his kiss on my neck before a sharp pain covered my body. I whimpered grabbing his hand which was around my neck and my tears surfaced.

"Why-" I whispered as my vision got burly.

"I promise you will not be hurt by me again after this." I heard him before the pain continued.

He was biting me, but the soft spot on my neck made it unbearable. And soon I felt as I my blood was falling out.

I shudder at the sudden feeling of arousal as he pulls away and kisses my lips. My body was now in his arms as I cried while he apologized. I could taste my blood on his lips.

With that, the doors to our chambers suddenly opened and I heard Lydia gasp before apologizing and running out. He chuckled watching the door closed and looking at me. I however was terribly embarrassed being under the King, both of us naked in such a position.

I stare down as he pulled me into him and let me rest my head on his chest before I fainted.

"Shall I tell you about things you might not know before you go ?"

I look at Maria, The Queen's primary ladies-in-waiting.

"What?" I asked softly with a curious gaze.

"Beware of the ones who have no wives."

I frown laughing in dubiety.

"They aren't human Ruby."

I stopped my chuckle and remembered where I was marrying off to.

"I heard they mark their wives. So all know she is taken."

"Mark how?" I asked

She was about to say but we were disturbed by a servant asking us to help the queen get dressed. I wish she told me that before I left.

I opened my eyes and my neck suddenly felt sore. I touch it shocked by how hot my skin was

"Madam. You are awake!" Lydia said helping me up and I realized I was now wearing clothes unlike when I woke up earlier.

I groan at the sudden headache," Uh, what, what happened?" I asked holding my head and feeling weak.

"Forgive me, Madam. I walked in. I didn't know."

I didn't care about it, all I could think of was my headache.

"Your Highness, a warm bath will help you with your sore neck and headache."

I look up to see Maya standing beside Lydia. Lydia helped me up as I look at the bath, the ladies now preparing for me.

"How did you know?" I asked as I walked towards it.

"You were marked this morning by the King, your highness of course we know."

I snap my head at her before letting Lydia take my gown off as the maids walked out.

Marked? That was a weird way to say my husband bit me and it was clearly visible.

"If you don't mind Madam, I would like to rub rose oil on your neck. It will help." Maya said grabbing a bottle filled with oil and showing me. I nodded before taking the gown completely off and getting in the hot bath.

Maya seemed like she knew about things that I or Lydia couldn't. It was important I ask her about it. I lay back and put my head on the pillow as Lydia put some oils in the bath with flowers. I smiled grabbing one and watching it while Maya rubbed my shoulders.

"We were told by the King to take extreme care of you My queen. We understood you might need some sleep so we didn't disturb you. However, it would be best for you to have a light meal and prepare for the ball."

Ah yes, the ball. She did mention it last night before leaving. A ball was held for the King and his Queen. Me. I was nervous to walk between them. They emitted a frightening strong aura and it scared me.

Not to mention these people were like a close community not liking any humans within them and here I was, Under their glares. I was the outsider. And I was sure I was hated a lot already.

I could feel it from the King's soldiers although talking to them helped put an ease on my nerves the same could not be said for the court and the Royals who resided within these walls.

They could very well hate me already just because I am human.

"What -" I pause to frame the question better. "How did you know my neck was sore?" I asked and Maya smiled handing me a mirror.

I stare at my neck, red and purple with a small scar where King Xerxes bit me. I didn't know it was that visible.

"My god" I breathe out.

"How?" I questioned this harsh bite.

"It is something we do your Highness, our mates mark us, you cannot be touched and if that man refuses to respect this mark. He is good as dead."

I look at Maya as she nodded.

"Why? Everyone must already know of the two yes?"

"It's the way of our Wolves.. this isn't just a mark you see. It's more like your presence is being altered. All men will know who you are now. And that is how it should be."

"So, the men in this kingdom just know who the woman is fated with by just a mark?"

Maya laughed humming in thought.

"No, not all. The alter in your presence can only be noticed if an Alpha has done so. Therefore, as the Alpha King has marked your highness. You will be seen as our Queen instantly. For us folks, it's more like they can tell if we have a mate, just not who-"

"Your Highness. The ball has begun." one of my ladies-in-waiting informed us and Maya nodded before carrying on her work.

I step out of the bath and I was wrapped in a cloth with my hair held up away from my wet back by Lydia, she helped me step out and I look back at my brush before wrapping the cloth around my body and grabbing my hair brush.

"It has been advised to be hostile to Sir Raymond. He is the ambassador of our kingdom. Here to represent us. You may only speak a few words not more than a sentence."

I look at Lydia, "Why should we be cold to people from our own kingdom?"

She sighs looking down while she applies perfume to my neck," That was to indicate you support this kingdom, you shall favour your new home over your past, you are the Queen now. Madam, you cannot spare any gossip."

I look back at the mirror in disappointment and keep brushing my hair. Suddenly the maids outside go quiet as they fussed with my gowns. I couldn't see since I was facing the mirror. Lydia suddenly bowed leaving me and I frown about to ask her by turning my head when I see him.

***

CHAPTER 16

I was in nothing but a piece of cloth covering my bits. My hair is fuzzy and curls falling to my bum. I brushed it staring at the mirror before it was pinned in an appropriate style for the ball. I was waiting in the cold for my maid to warm up my petticoat with the help of fire so I could feel warm inside.

I wanted to sit and have something to eat.. Perhaps some fruit before I was wrapped up in those huge gowns and jewels and sent out in the crowd of hundreds of people. People who hated humans. Like me.

But when I felt the room so silent. I watched as Maya walked out with others and Lydia held my petticoat before noticing something and keeping it on the chair beside the mantle and leaving.

My brows creased in confusion till I felt his eyes on me.

My heart almost froze seeing The King behind me through the mirror. As I stood in a thin bathcloth covering my body, I suddenly felt shivers run up my body as every part of me now was highly sensitive. He had not seen all of me yet. I knew that, standing almost naked before him made my core clenched.

I felt hot... Hotter as he slowly walked towards me. His eyes never left mine and I turned to him. My hair brushed still in my hands and I held it to my chest. Possibly trying to hide my sudden erect buds poking through that thin wet fabric.

He wasn't in formal attire yet.

The ball had started but the maids never rushed to get me ready so I assumed we didn't have to attend yet.

He wore a simple shirt and trousers. Something all men wore when not outside their homes. His hair was wet. His skin was radiant. I could smell a lavender on him indicating that the King had already taken a bath.

But he was supposed to be getting ready in his chambers.

Why was he here, before me...making it so hard for me to breath.

There was a moment of silence between us a moment where I saw his eyes glance at my body and somehow show anger. Till he trapped me between the table and his chest. My hands were digging into my chest as they pushed back.

He touched the top of my hairbrush and tingles shot right up my core, He didn't even touch me. Yet I was feeling as if I was getting eaten out by a beast.

His eyes stayed on my face but mine dropped to his chest. I couldn't dare look up. He was far too intimidating. He seemed angry or seemed as if any word spoken would anger him.

"Why are you covering yourself with a hairbrush? " He asked taking it out of my hands and putting it down on the table behind me.

I gulp the non-existent words down my throat. His chest pushed on mine more as his face dropped. His cheek rubbed against mine and I felt his light beard tickle my jaw. His lips suddenly touched my ears and I held back a sudden moan to protect my embarrassing expression. I should be as good as a melting pile of cream if he didn't stop.

"How dare you cover what's mine, Ruby? "

That was a threat. That was a threat!

My eyes went wide in fear as his palm rested on my waist and squeezed my skin.

"I can smell your fear. "

I close my eyes shut, tight and held back yet another moan as his breath tickled my ear lobe. His lips brushed gently like a feather over my sensitive ear lobe causing me to push my legs together and pray I didn't make any unwanted noise.

I didn't want to know what was next. I just wanted my core to stop throbbing. I wanted my body to stop trembling in a sort of aroused fear-like state.

I was scared. Immensely, I dare not deny it. But I was aroused by his touch.

I was still very much uncomfortable around him. I didn't know how to act. I remembered how he had kissed me. Seen my body. Touched me. But I was sure it would take me a lot of time to get used to our close proximity.

"Why are you in wet clothes, in such cold weather? " He asked pulling away and looking down.

I could see his eyes darken as he saw my skin peek through that wet cloth.

My tongue was caught. And he did not like it. And I paid for it. He grabbed my jaw harshly and tilted my head up to meet his gaze earning a whispered cry from me.

"I asked you multiple questions yet you decide to stay quiet? Is that how you wish to be? "

I tried to jerk my head violently but in vain as I couldn't quite move it much considering his rough hand was pinning my jaw to stand straight and dare my eyes to look anywhere but in his eyes.

"I was waiting for them to warm my petticoat. And" I paused slightly,"I - I always brush my hair before I get d-dressed"

He frowned in confusion.

"Why? "

" I don't know. I-It's a habit? I suppose."

I did stumble across my words. I stumbled a lot. While I explained. King Xerxes began to undo my damp cloth And it fell to my feet, catching me off guard, exposing me to the cold air and making me shiver. I had instinctively pulled my arms around my bare chest before I could even think. But one look suddenly I was pulling them back down. As If I just knew his command.

How curious...How could I just do as his eyes commanded? How could I just give in to his expression?

He didn't hide his gaze. His eyes dropped from mine to my neck. His fingers traced the mark he had given me. His eyes wander down to my breasts, still perky and refusing to go down. The cold air brushed against them making them even harder.

I almost gasped as his hands rested on my waist. They were extremely hot. So hot I felt as if he could warm me up better than the fire itself.

I bit my lip as he let his fingers rub over my skin. My hands rested over his chest in fists as they had nowhere else to go. I was scared of moving and getting him angry but I didn't want to be devoid of that touch either.

But I moved my hands to rest on his large, muscular, rock hard...I was getting carried away.

Biceps...Never had I seen such large arms that could possibly carry a huge wood log individually.

I had a thing for them. Not just his. I always liked watching men train in the courtyards. Their arms are clearly defined.

But they were nothing.. Compared to the man who stood before me. My arms were like a twig before his.

I squeaked audibly as he suddenly grabbed my right breast, catching me out of my bubble as making my knees wobbly, again!

"How are they so big and soft?"

What...?

I blushed, I felt my neck heat up right there. His eyes were filled with lust and fascination. As he rubbed his hand and squeezed it I would softly cry out feeling a wet pool between my legs while I covered my mouth with the back of my hand and looked away embarrassed and shy. He seemed to enjoy the results of his actions on me, as his lips would slightly curl up every time my body reacted to it. His eyes would show a glint of happy satisfaction when he heard my soft cries and gasps to his sudden touches. I digress, but I knew this was his way of a tease.

He suddenly clenched his jaw throwing me over his shoulders and walking to my bed.

"My king.. You have to be.. Be-" I sucked in a deep breath as he licked my neck and his tongue went straight down to my breasts.

He squeezed me and pinched me while his mouth latched onto my bud. But then he took it in his mouth, all whilst staring right at me. Telling me what he was capable of.Pulling away only to catch my bud between his teeth and let go for it to jiggle, he was amused and I couldn't for the life of me stop him.

His eyes widened as he squeezed both my breasts.

Had he never had a woman with a bigger bust in bed?

I blushed as he ran his thumb over my nipple and his tongue licked it earning a loud moan from me.

"So fucking soft"

I cried out loud as he squeezed them too tight making it hurt. He let go as he heard me.

"Too much? " he asked nuzzling his head in my neck.

I was practically unable to, at this point breathe, think, move, talk or even keep my eyes open. I was so absorbed in the haze.

I shook my head lightly as he asked me a question, I didn't want him to think I hated it. I liked it, I couldn't think of being devoid of his touch, I would possibly go mad. And then, the chance to carry my duty as the queen would turn into a battlefield.

Not that I was only letting him do it for the sake of my duty. He called me his mate. Something they cannot call just anyone.

I knew that word carried a heavy weight.

And I couldn't deny how I felt with him.

"We.. Have to.. " I barely get a few words out as he dips his head down to take both my ni*ples in his mouth.

"Sir! " I yelled out suddenly.

I didn't know why. I just didn't want to call him by his name yet.

He let go of my poor ni*ples. They are all red and hot now. He stared at me as my chest was heaving and my eyes were watery because of all the heat.

"I liked that." He said before getting up.

I gasp as he swings his arms under me and picks me up carrying me to my powder room and setting me on the chair and standing before me, Might I add, still naked before him?

His hand suddenly cupped my cheek and chin slowly tilting my head to look at him. To say this was one of the most erotic positions I was in. Sitting before him while his manhood was almost at my mouth while he held my chin.

I wanted to slap myself at how naughty my thoughts were.

"Keep your hair down-" His voice turned husky, it made me clench my legs together and look away.

"And wear red".

|| CHAPTER 17 ||

I looked at myself in the mirror turning around to see my back and satisfied.I asked them to change the dress. I was to wear a dark green gown under the Queen Dowager's order. But when I mentioned his desire for Maya she immediately switched my dress.

I wonder if this was a part of the protocol. The king had the final say in everything. Not the mother. But in our kingdom, the Queen Mother was a highly influential part of the protocol.

I wonder what kind of women she was, occupied in my own thoughts as Maya fussed around me making sure I looked perfect she asked me if it was to my liking.

My neck only carried one simple white pearl choker. My ears had pearl drops and my hands were covered with white gloves and the wedding ring over them. The red velvet dress hugged my waist perfectly. The cold outside was freezing but the dress hugged me perfect to give the warmth needed, however it came with the price of my tight corset, even thought it fit me perfectly, I preferred a tighter one.I was so accustom to tighter busts I had it measure an inch smaller to make my waist more slim. It puffed perfectly below my waist. I was very much thankful that the front hem of my dress was just above my toes.

I had no chance of tripping over it.

"Thank you," I said looking at my maids and searching for Lydia.

"Lydia? " I asked.

" I shall be beside you for the entire night. Forgive me but Miss Lydia has yet to learn all our rules."

Maya explained as the other bowed and left the chamber.

"No problem. But where is-"

"Madam-" She walked in with a black box.

I almost gasped in relief.

"Thank you. I wondered where all the boxes were" I said opening the box and taking my grandmother's gold chain out.

I wore it but tucked the rest In my bust. It was too long.

Maya frowned, "I am very sorry madam I had no idea you wished to wear this as well. I would've kept the box ready and had your jewels polished."

I smile shaking my head.

"It's alright. "

Sir Andrew stood before the halls leading to our chamber. Waiting to escort me.He always had a neutral look just like the king. He was very much hard to read not to mention had a frightening aura around.

He held his forearm out and I placed my hand over his. With Maya behind us, we walked down to the North wing of the castle with three guards and one butler escorting us.

I heard our footsteps click over the marble floor and for some reason, the sound calmed me down

As we walked towards the huge ballroom door. I gulp and my body goes almost limp seeing the King. He stood with his back to me. His cape Black with gold boarders. The King's waldrop was devoid of any colours except the dark.

His hair was now brushed back. His robes all black but his shirt was white. He looked occupied in thoughts for me to speak. So I stood behind him, silent, not wanting to disturb his chain of thoughts and in fear he might not appreciate my greeting.

"Your majesty. " One of the knights I saw with the king perviously walked to him.

"Sir Fredrick wishes to speak with you about some matters. He requests an audience. "

I snap my head at that man hearing Fred's name, I wanted to see him. The one man from my home and I had not seen him causing a great deal of anxiety. My heavy earrings clinked grabbing the King's attention. He snapped his eyes back at the man and nodded.

"Grant an audience during the dinner"

The king didn't bother looking at them again. He simply turned to me and wrapped his hand around my waist. I stumble closer to him blushing with multiple sets of eyes on us.

He leaned in, his lips pressed to my ear. His mouth was now hidden from others and on my neck and he gave a slight kiss before bringing his lips back to my ear lobe.

While the King appeared so nonchalant, I on the other hand was already seeing fog surrounding my mind, I would fluster and stiffen up every time his lips came near me, I could already feel my legs weaken.

"You look beautiful in red, Ruby"

I couldn't tell myself how warm bubbly and hot I felt hearing that. It made my heart swell up.

I was happy the king was pleased with me. I wanted nothing but to be sure of not making a fool out of myself in this fearsome court.

He held out his hand and I soft laced mine in his elbow as we walked out. Unlike our traditions. The King and Queen never walked out between many of the subjects.

Unless it was an informal ball. We were on a balcony. Much different and grand than the ballroom I remember back in my kingdom...

My kingdom...

I lower my gaze remembering I can no longer say that.

We acknowledged the crowd before sitting at the large table behind us that looked upon the bustling crowds and the never-ending cues of dances.

The women endowed luxurious gown which shined under the massive chandeliers, they looked so beautiful. The crowd, from esteemed families and royals blending in with their people. I gulp at uncomfortable stares of some, I felt isolated, alone. The only one who wasn't suppose to be here, the one who didn't belong. I didn't speak, instead focused on the food and wine before me.

Why not enjoy the one thing you were given ?

The King didn't speak much. Only talked to his advisor about finances and conflicts happening within the primary city while concurrently greeting the members of court as they presented themselves before us.

"We have a report from the border. It seemed that one of the villages was destroyed because of dispersed." I heard Andrew's whisper.

The king snapped his eyes at the advisor.

"Dispersers? "

I looked away not wanting to hear them instead staring at the glass of wine, grabbing it and taking a sip. To my shock it was good.

I happily chew on the delicious food but elegantly while I drown the next glass of wine.

This one didn't make me hot and feel like I was gonna faint at all!

I smile. I knew that the wine I had back at the first ball was not to my taste.

"My King, Lord Clark is here to greet your Majesty's"

The king leaned back staring at the messenger as he stepped aside revealing a man. Blonde hair, sharp eyes and his mouth held a smirk. He bowed, his eyes on me as I squirmed in my seat while the King turned to take a glass.

"Your Majesty's. It is a pleasure to meet you, My Queen"

The way he said that didn't quite settle well when there was tension between us all. I smiled nodding.

"First ever Human Queen of our family. How beautiful. "

I frown in my head at that comment.

"He is the youngest of my father's siblings. Clark Vincent. You may go" The king stated with a neutral tone.

He smiled bowing and his eyes looked at me once before he turned to leave.

I gulp looking away, feeling like he hated me Or something.

I did envy the people dancing thou. I loved dancing. But I suppose the King wasn't fond of it. As I lean back in my chair and slowly drink from the glass. My eyes stare out at the view of men and women. Their beautiful gown flowed as they danced and their jewels shone through the floor.

I unconsciously touched the chain on my neck.

I see Fredrick step into the room and I smile looking at him as he bows before us.

He was holding a heavy-looking file.

Chapter No edited*

|| CHAPTER 18 ||

I loved dancing. But I suppose the King wasn't fond of it. As I lean back in my chair and slowly drink from the glass. My eyes stare out at the view of men and women. Their beautiful gown flowed as they danced and their jewels shone through the floor.

Unconsciously touching my chain,I see Fredrick step into the room and I smile looking at him as he bows before us.

He was holding a heavy-looking file.

His eyes seemed to stare down at me so I looked up at him in confusion but the King's hand extended to grab mine, as I realized my fuzzy head was slowing down, I fussed to keep the wine glass down and grab his hand.

As I stood up, my vision moved. I blink seeing everything blurry and my gut drops.

Did I drink too much?

I didn't remember how many times my glass was filled.

My nerves were at the edge while he escorted me down the stairs. My hand pulled up the dress and Maya was behind me helping me.

We stood at the doors of the ballroom where everyone was gathered and my heartbeat quickened.

We were going to dance? Why didn't anyone tell me? I felt heavy-headed. I was drunk to be exact.

My eyes shut closed with a visible frown because of my worry.

"Ruby."

My eyes snapped up to the King as he watched me raise my eyebrows a bit to question his call. His hand left mine and wrapped around my waist.

Oh my god! oh my god. I was to dance before his people, half drunk. What if I tripped? what if. My thoughts were interrupted as he glanced at me once. The hall on the other side went silent, I could already feel the eyes of people on us and whispers around.

I could suddenly feel the heat creeping into my veins, my legs pushed together feeling tingling in my stomach. His touch was overwhelming. It worsened the effect of alcohol in me.

His other hand took mine and the doors opened.

I felt cold. But my body was hot. As they all looked at me I felt a sense of dread rush to me. Their eyes carried a lot of anger.

How could the Queen of our Clan be a human?

I was sure that's what they were thinking.

They all bow, the women curtsey before us. But for their King. Not to me. They would never bow to a human. After all, it was us who came on our knees for their kind.

My mind was in a haze as he moved to the centre of the room. Under the beautiful huge chandelier filled with jewels.

My hands trembled with the nervous state and got sweaty. I didn't get the chance to wipe them as he pulled me into his chest and took my hand. Holding my waist tight.

The music started slowly as we slowly danced among the people, gossip from ladies and men filled the room and then I felt the room get dim for me.

My heartbeat quickened its pace as he spun me. Butterflies fluttered in my stomach every time his hand wrapped around my waist. When his cheek intentionally brushed against mine, his thumb would rub up and down my torso. His eyes, frozen on me putting me in a tight spotlight.

I danced as well as my body would let me. I had done that since I was a kid. I was easy when my mind wasn't filled with worry. But today it was, and I did my best to ignore it.

As I looked around while our legs moved along the floor, His face flashed across my eyes. The day when The Prince took my hand and guided me across the floor. Declaring his wish to marry me. We dance between our people, seeing smiles on their faces. I realized how my mind has diverted to a memory that should no longer be important. I chuck it away immediately.

A memory which was dear to me, but would be inappropriate to think of as married women.

"Your eyes seem much more interested in others than me."

I jerk my head up to him, scared of his taunt.

"I would prefer if you looked into my eyes than others. Or do I need to command you to do so?"

It was a command which simply could not be rejected. When I dared to lift my gaze up , I was greeted with sullen face.

Did he not like my behaviour? But I was quiet. The whole night I did nothing to anger him.

"Are you unwell? " He asked as I shook my head.

"No... No."

"Then? "

I gasped as he lifted me, spun before setting me down, my bust touched his mouth slightly as he lowered me down, something I couldn't forget, and but he continued with the dance effortlessly while I was left feeling multiple different emotions. Some gasps around the room echo. It seemed that they had never seen their King take the floor before.

"I asked you a question Ruby."

The fear hovering over me worsened.

"Lot of p- people. " I whisper.

Silence. After his question was what he hated. And I had done it many times.

I saw the content in his eyes as I answered him. I had a lot on my mind, but I chose to keep my remarks strictly towards the people surrounding us.

"There are a lot of people in attendance today." I continued.

"Do you not like dancing? "

My eyes widen and I immediately rush to answer, "No! No I-I I love dancing. You are a great dancer as well Your Majesty"

I hide my stutter and nervous state with a compliment to his graceful steps.

"Good to hear," He said.It seemed that the music was slow on purpose. I could feel his hands on me. I could feel him push me closer every minute and soon I felt his lips lightly brush against my cheek causing my vision to blur.

Had I always been this sensitive to a man's touch? I never felt this way when the Prince took my hand. Was I because was comfortable with him? But I didn't hate the King's touch.

This thought had been running in my mind all day.

My hands felt sweaty inside my glows now, they felt hot, I didn't like that. I sigh as we ended our dance and my head lowered with a curtsey to His Majesty. But he didn't let of my hand. Had I not kept my head running I might just be fainting by now.

A tiny smile I gave to the Royal family who stood across us and I curtsey before looking up to them. All staring and clapping with expressions I could not name.

"To the King! and our Queen! "

Said the Ambassador of the kingdom. I heard the clinking of glasses before the chatter began, Charlie Williams the ambassador smiled at us grabbing another glass of the tray. I looked at him while he walked towards us with two glasses and offered one to me.

I nervously chuckled taking the glass in my hand, The king glanced at me in a curious gaze once before raising his glass and drinking.

I am fucked... Utterly.

I couldn't stop smiling. Because I was truly drunk. I had forgotten some wines can get you drunk after a while. And I had happily emptied 4 or 5 of them. And now here I was. Sipping on champagne. I wonder if I would puke.

I hope not.

I hold back my laugh. I was laughing at myself. Enjoying my happy time before It crashes down. From to tomorrow. I was going to see the reality of my life.

My thoughts were yet again interrupted by him, That man's hand had some magic. How could he just make my body freeze? Including my brain.

As felt a squeeze on my other hand and I realized my hand was still in his.

No wonder it was sweaty and hot, and possibly burning inside.

"Ruby..."

"Y-" I had to clear my throat first,"Yes Your Majesty? "

He stared at me for quite a while before looking behind me. I frown glancing behind us as he wraps his hand. Again! Again! Around my waist.

Can't you see this was a torture to my nerves? His hand was too much for my poor body.

He suddenly took the glass from my hand and stared at it with wide eyes noticing it to be almost empty. Just a few sips felt.

When did I drink that?

"Come," he said, pushing me towards the doors of ball room.

We walked through the parted crowd towards the stairs leading up to the balcony.

The fresh cold air hits my face I take an audible deep breath. Warm visible air comes out of my mouth as I exhale.

He wrapped his hand around my shoulder, it was very hot, the hand. And him... How could he be so warm? Ah yes, we just danced. I glanced at him once and saw anger again. Plastered over his face as always.

Does he ever let his face relax?

I bite my lip as he dragged me toward the back area where I could see no one. The guards stood at the entrance making me blink and question why were we here until he cupped my cheeks catching me off guard and pushed me to lean against the baluster.

My stomach felt like it erupted in fireworks. There was nothing I could find to describe my feelings when he had me cornered like so. It was overwhelming.

I suck in cold air and he had trapped me between the railings and his chest. His body is dangerously close to mine. I could feel his warmth on me as he pressed his torso on my chest.

Scratch that. He was glued to me.

I could feel my nether reign heat up and pool.

"You are flushed red. Burning."

|| CHAPTER 19 ||

"H uh.."

It wasn't a question. I knew I was burning up. It was the wine of course. His voice shocked me. Throughout the night he spoke with such authority and an intimidating tone. It was rough, to point and fearful. Yet this time as he talked to me it was calm, stern but soft.

I had my hand on the baluster. It slips making my shoulder drop and he wrapped his arm around my waist and I nearly felt my knees give in.

"Ruby " He dragged my name in a whisper as his mouth came closer.

Oh, Lord. I would melt right here. My body would turn into liquid and be vaporized that minute.

I didn't want to close my eyes. I liked his neck. It was dangerously close to my mouth and for some reason, I wanted a bite.

But he was the King. I pouted with discontent as he leaned back, I noticed his eyes go wide at me.

"You a drunk? "

I dread his stringent remarks, Biting my lip and looking afar to show my dejection however his hand was much faster to bring it right back where it was.

"Yes. Your majesty. I-I had wine. Forgive me for making a fool out of myself"

I was trying to be formal. But it somehow came out as a childish tone.

I sensed my breathing getting heavy and hot.I squint my eyes at that feeling.

He wrapped his arms around me preventing my head from hitting to hard on his chest. I was far to gone by now but I could make out the sound of the balcony doors open.

Ahh... to my my maid.

She rushed to us and draped a red warm shawl over my shoulder.

Ahh... That felt better. Much better.

The king slowly led me to the couch to our left and helped me sit down. I flop my body back unable to sit straight anymore as my eyes see the sky completely forgetting who I was, who I was with and how I should have behaved.

Ahh... I made a fool of myself.

I am drunk. Possibly would say something that would be the dead of me. I tittered seeing the King glance at me once and I covered my mouth looking away and he walked away from me.

I sigh... "That's what you get for trying to enjoy your life Ruby" I whisper.

Now.. He has seen how undesirable I was and now. I would be abandoned.

I stare at the beautiful sky and smile hugging my arms together.

To my shock he walked back to me, sitting down before resting his hand on the back of my head, while I sat there with the heartbeat of a horse running.

He was leaning down enough close that just me moving an inch would touch our lips.

He sighs... His hair strands fell over his eyes and I feel my heart flutter.

Oh, what a gorgeous face he had. All ladies in the kingdom must swoon over him. Not to mention most of them, eligible princesses.

Oh gosh... He was too beautiful for me. He suddenly clears his throat and looked away.. His eyes glanced at the doors of the balcony and then at me.

"Come. You need sleep. " He said taking off his coat and putting it on my lap.

"Could- May I look at the sky for a while longer? My maid could escort me back to my chambers"

He seemed to be taken aback at my request but said nothing. I thought he would leave. But he instead sat beside me.

We stare at the sky and I smile. This was one thing peaceful to look at other than nature.

"They are like diamonds. " I said and chuckled.

I sensed his shift and suddenly his arms wrapped behind my back and pulled me closer to him. His other took mine and squeezed it.

"Does it hurt? " He asked and I looked at him.

"What? " I asked since in my hazy state.

But I was much more aroused I just couldn't do anything in fear of being rejected. I wanted to sit on his lap for some reason.

I slapped myself in my head.

" Your chest... Does it not hurt because of the corset? "

My head falls down. My eyes stared at my bust. My Boussom is half out and my hand comes up to cover it.

I had no idea they pushed together like that when I sat down. I suddenly remember pushing the dress down since the sequined neckline hurt my skin.

"Do not - " He paused, "Cover yourself before me. It might just entice to me rip that off"

I gasped as he grabbed my hand pulling on it and pulling my body with it. I landed on his chest. Like an idiot..

"I don't like you covering yourself before me"

Oh Lord, do I feel shy?

Because I looked down and leaned back sitting properly as he let go of my hand.

"N-no... It doesn't hurt- I should asked them to leave the trim out."

" Did the maids lace it too tight then?" He asked.

Eh... Ehh... What is he doing?

I gulp pressing my back to the couch as he brings his hand to my chest and his fingers hook on my neckline and pull it.

He stares at my cleavage before His finger traces the lining, to feel it I suppose. While his nonchalant self continued to feel my skin under his finger, My attentive mind was trying its best to stop the state of arousal I was in.

"Do I need to change your maids? The dress doesn't seem comfortable.. "

"No! ... It's... Ment to be so. If it was too loose I suppose my Boussom would fall out"

Goodness, look at my informal tone. That was the hill to the void.

He stared at me as I chuckled. No words, yet his finger was still hooked on the neckline of my dress right between my breasts might I add.

"Very well then, as long you are comfortable" He whispered.

The only response I could give as he suddenly kissed my neck was to bite my own lip, to stop myself from shrieking and moaning. Right below my ear, my eyes closed shut as his lips traced his kisses down to my collar.

I had unconsciously grabbed his wrists... Squeezing it. I could ascertain the smirk on my skin as his other hand cupped my jaw and tilted my head.

I yelped with a shudder as he licked my neck and I pushed myself away unable to digest that feeling.

"I.. We... People.. " my words were a bundle of stutters which were unable to form a sentence as he ignored them, continuing his light assault.

I held my breath trying to hold back a gasp as he picked me up. I couldn't find the strength to keep my head up as the guards watched their king in shock as he carried me inside.

My head dipped and pushed into his chest as he effortlessly walked with long strides towards our chambers.

He set me down on the bed and there was a minute of silence as Maya walked in with hot towels for us. She sets it down as The King looks out the window away from us while unhooking his shirt.

I gulp as she peeks up to see what he is doing and she looks at me with a frown.

What? What was she looking at me for?

‖ CHAPTER 20 ‖

I raised my eyebrows as she slowly got up and cleared her throat. He doesn't move.

She then kneels before me and helps me take off my shoes. Those dreaded shoes. I loved them but my feet couldn't agree. I wince at the pain in my heels and push the dress down.

I was bleary in fact, I couldn't think straight.

I watched the king in fear as he took off his shirt and flung it over the couch before the mantle while Maya undid my hair. I felt better as the ornaments were taken off my head.

"Miss, can you move? " She asked softly.

"You call your queen that? "

We both snapped our heads at King Xerxes, his voice booming through the whole chamber and she immediately went on her knees shaking her head.

I flinch at his tone myself, keeping my hand over her shoulder and reassuring her of no harm.

"Forgive me your Majesty's. " She apologises profusely as the king walks just a few steps ahead with a glass of brown liquid. His face held disappointment and earth.

"If you can't address her as your Queen, you might well be exiled for your indecorum" He stated nonchalantly raising the glass to his lips.

I couldn't dare speak but when I saw her trembling in fear I couldn't take it.

"I.. " My tongue was caught. My eyes widen as he looks at me. My heart fell. He looked frightening, with a macabre look in those eyes of his, I could see why people feared this man.

"I asked her to call me that." I almost choked saying that.

"Did you? Or are you trying to save her? "

Why was he so rude?

I frown looking at him with Maya still on the ground. On her knees.

"No. I got tired of everyone calling me by my title all day. She is one of my primary maids. I gave her permission."

I see his left brow raise as he sets his glass down.

"Out"

She immediately stood up and bowed before scurrying out. The door closes and I see dread fill my body.

He was angry no doubt. And I had now made it worse. I sit there, frozen in worry, twisting the fabric of my dress in my hands.

"Get up"

He commands, walking to me. I take a deep breath before standing up but my legs gave in. My vision became blurred as I felt myself sway and almost fall before he caught me.

I could feel my body press against his and his warmth engulfed me like a blanket. I chuckled... For some reason. Feeling tickles on my neck. When I opened my eyes ever so slightly. I was in his arms, being carried.

I snapped my neck up as he carried me to the powder room. His effortless strength made me feel like I would swoon over him every day.

Oh.. Yes. I was swooning.

I bite my tongue and stay still as he sets me down on the chair before my vanity.

"I didn't know my wife loved drinking. "

I gulp shaking my head side to side and looking down as he moved my hair across my back to my right.

His fingers linger on my neck just for a while, before he unhooks the necklace and sets it down over the vanity counter.

I gulp closing my eyes as he leans down, anymore of him I could not afford to see. It was simple too much. His lips pressed against my ear before I felt him take my earrings off. I had jerked my head away only slightly out of shock but I could feel his disapproving look through my shut eyes.

My eyes opened in disbelief and embarrassment as I feel my laces being undone from the back. For a women, to have her laces undone by a man was an obscene act.

Even if he was my husband, I felt shy. As if it was something bad.

I lick my lips taking the dress off but only over my torso. My cream corset and thin petticoat are now exposed.

"So beautiful"

I heard him as he undid my corset. I was in fear he might be annoyed with all those laces. But he was slow. He seemed to find his amusement in plucking each of them individually.

I felt it loosen and it dropped down before I pressed my hand on my chest. I take a sigh. Feel it come off me almost forgetting who was undressing me.

I didn't remember taking my hand off my chest.

My petticoat was see-through. I blush embarrassed. But when I saw my face in the mirror. I was even more flustered. My face was red, My neck was red, my hair was fuzzy. I looked like a mess!

And him... I saw him in all his naked glory.

When did he take his trousers off?

I had no idea... And I didn't mind seeing that line stretch from his sides to..

Oh my god..

I snap my eyes back down to my legs.

"Up"

I tried to avoid my eyes from falling over that. But I couldn't because he walked right in front of me. He grabbed my hand and pulled me up.

My obedience was laughable, It came so naturally to me.

When my chest brushed against his and I saw him close his eyes and tilt his head back before wrapping his hands behind my back. I liked the hug. I was enjoying the hug.

Till I feel my dress fall on the floor and the cold air brushed past my body. I shiver in his arms.Making him nuzzle his head in my neck.

"Have I made you angry? "

My tongue seemed to talk on its own now.

"No" That was a curt reply.

"Then why do youuuu seem angry! "

Why was it like this? To me... I was talking properly. But then I heard myself. How could l slur my words before the King?

The KING!

I slapped my hands on my mouth, my heart beating fast as he stared down at me with his dark eyes. I took this as a sign to accept his wrath. He seemed the type of man to kill people over a simple joke. No humor.

As I made the daring move to stare at his eyes, I noticed a thin white scar over his temple at the right. I wonder how he got so many scars, his body was covered in them. Battles? Or perhaps training?

"I am not angry "

His soft voice reaches my ear.. pulling my eyes down to his lips. When he puts his hand on the back of my waist and leans down. His lips purposefully brush past my neck before he pulls away.

"No? "I pout asking. I forgot I had to stay quiet.

He doesn't answer. I feel my corset drop down and my petticoat suddenly take off. I stood naked before him yet again bare, hot and yet cold altogether

I gulp pulling my arms together to cover my breasts but.. It didn't help. They were big enough not to be covered by my hands. I look down, embarrassed yet again.

He seemed to have this impossible effect on me. Making me feel nervous, shy, scared, and unable to keep my mind at ease.

I sucked in the cold air as his finger reached to my chest, he grabbed the pendant of my chain and stared.

If I could say, I felt his touch over my skin even though his finger nearly touched me, I wouldn't be able to put in the right words to describe the feeling it gave.

The sheer ability of this man to make me feel before he did it was incredible. His aura was incredible. It aroused me, and made me feel stupid.

|| CHAPTER 21||

"I do not remember gifting you this. "

My eyes peer at him. He remembered every piece of jewellery he gave me at the wedding.

"It belonged to my grandmother"

A soft nod was what he replied with, making me nervous when he slowly took it off me. His hand brushed over my chest and it throbbed under that finger, he threw me over his shoulder earning a loud gasp from me and taking me aback. I felt nothing but embarrassed as he made his way towards the bath and all I could see was his rear end.

He picked me up like a sack of potatoes, so unconcerned by his own actions. His whole personality revolved around being unapologetic. And still, I found it humorous. A man who did not care about anything but getting what he wanted, seemed curious and intriguing.

Many of the ladies would find this displeasing. Being touched without showing softness before. I suppose there was something wrong with me. As I quite enjoyed his manhandling ways with me.

My stomach flipped as he set me down near the bathtub.

I didn't have to question. I knew what he wanted. I sniffed softly because of my runny nose and slowly got in. My body relaxed in the hot water and the chilly shivers over my body disappeared.

He got in behind me and he made himself comfortable before pulling me by my waist into him. I sat with my nerves constantly on edge between his huge legs. His hands are around my waist and I feel the hot water drip down my scape. I closed my eyes at the warm feeling.

Pushing my now wet hair on my side so it wasn't stuck to his chest he guides me to lay my back on his chest. I couldn't just sit in that uncomfortable position but feeling his chest on my back seemed more erotic than just comfortable. With his arms around me and me trying to get away wasn't an option.

I had a pull towards him. And although I hated being a part of that treaty. He had respected me. I liked him. And he made me feel attached.

Like I wouldn't find anyone else like him. Perhaps it was because he was the only man whom I could depend on for my future. I didn't believe in their beliefs. I wasn't one of them. But... It was unusual for a human to get attached to someone like this. Surely there was something wrong with me.

My eyes opened and I sat up immediately as I felt a hard thing poke my bum. My hands cover my mouth as I turn around to see him eyeing me with anger.

Oh lord....

"S-sorry"

"Get. Back. Here" He commanded with his clenched teeth causing me to go back like an obedient pet. But this time his hard pressing right up my rare.

My core tensed so did my body as his finger traced my back. My neck, down till my waist, his fingers wrapping around my torso and his thumb softly rubbing up and down.

" How do you feel? " He asked kissing my neck.

If he wants me to answer properly, he shouldn't distract me. I tried to get my words out but my body was too overwhelmed by his lips tracing over my neck and back.

"I asked you a question, Ruby"

That was a threat.

My name, him calling me like that felt like a way to make sure I wouldn't defy him. And it did work.

"G-good. Forgive me if I made a fool out of myself. I didn't know how much I had. "

"You didn't"

I nodded. I was still very much drunk. But the hot bath calmed me down.

I turn just a bit to see him lean back and I hesitate before I let my finger touch his collar. He seemed to freeze almost making his skin taut under my finger. Not like me. More like a grunt and his body jerked back slightly.

I wasn't completely aware of my actions. The alcohol in me let me do what I wouldn't do normally, which was enjoy that steaming body under my fingers. I wanted to see how it felt it.

Didn't disappoint.

I traced my fingers over his chest, over his scars, going down his pecks to his torso before he stopped my hand.

I feared he didn't like me touching him. That he didn't allow it. But as he guides my hand to press completely against his beating heart. I felt myself come to ease.

I had no more strength to hear his heart as it caused my heart to beat faster and it was unbearable. I grabbed the wash clothes from the table beside the tub.

Perhaps I could distract my mind by doing something.

Holding it scrunched in my hand and lifting it to show him, " May I? " I asked softly.

He nodded and I slowly washed his neck. My hands moved down to his chest and stopped.

"You have to do it properly.." He said making me bite my lower lip to stop my smile.

As I took my hands further down to his lower torso line, I saw him close his eyes and sigh. But I never touched him below that. I was scared of it.

Too big..who knew what he'd do to me if I did touch it? Perhaps take me to bed...

I burst my bubble and blinked away those atrocious thoughts.

Bad! Very bad Ruby

I rubbed the washcloth over his legs before grabbing some lavender oil. I was busy rubbing it between my palms when he squeezed my waist tight.

"Ah! " That sounded so wrong.

I blush feeling flutters in my stomach as he picked me up and manoeuvred my legs on either side. Having me sit on his lap. Straddling him.

Ah yes, Before I could feel it on my back now I can feel it, right there. I could feel my insides clench.

His brow raised slightly, a subtle grin, daring me to continue and then I looked down at my mistake. His eyes dug into my soul, his hands squeezing my waist while I, I acknowledged my mistake and wondered how my body and mind could ever work together with this man around me.

"Sorry"

"Apologies should be backed by actions. " He says grabbing the washcloth cloth and placing it over my neck.

I sucked in a deep breath as he moved it from my neck to my back. He pulled me closer, A feeling better than just anything I ever felt.

I felt the hot cloth drag against my lower back and then come to my stomach before his hand came right up to my Boussom.

He didn't stop. Letting my moan out as he touched my breasts. The only barrier was that cloth.

That darn cloth.

I was shocked myself by thinking that.

He rubbed it over my me till he dragged it over my nip*les and I winced catching him off guard. His eyes snapped to mine telling of his concern.

He looked worried.

"They.... They can be sensitive sometimes" My whisper, my words were messed up. Any minute now, I would faint under his stare and hold and there I would leave my face in embarrassment.

I was blushing red in a bad way. I could tell.

"I see, Then my hand should be enough"

I didn't understand that.

"Huh? " Before I could comprehend he had dropped that cloth and grabbed my breasts.

"Oh !"

Doing something out of nowhere was of second nature to this man.

I moaned out loud as he squeezed them and brushed his thumb over my nipples making me squirm.

"Aren't you going to put that on me? "

What?

His eyes look at my hands covered in oil, Oh lord if I could run and hide my face.

His lips kissed my cheek pulling me close by squeezing them and pulling me by my breasts. I cry out softly at that sensual feeling. Rubbing my hands over his neck and massaging him as he stared at me making me want to hide in the corner.

His stare was making me squirm.

I would occasionally moan stopping my hands and biting my lips as he brushed his fingers over my nip**e while playing with my breasts.I gasped, crying out softly as he pinched them.

"That... That's too much " I moan out.

"Did I ask you to stop baby? "

My stomach filled with twists and turns as he said that.

Continuing my massage over his rock-hard shoulders I felt my wrists hurt. So I moved to his neck again rubbing my fingers over his skin and he tilted his head back.

His body was so hard and his chest was like a wall.

I yelp out while he pulled my ni*ple and let go. My hands snapped back and covered my breasts. My lips rolled back in my mouth as I looked down.

"I can't help it"

His husky voice said as he leaned toward me and pulled me much closer to his face. His hand pushed my hands aside guiding them back to his neck.

I was waiting for something. Maybe a kiss. Perhaps one of his antics of making me blush or squirm feeling my core tingle.

But he closed his eyes and dropped his head on my chest. I jerk slightly feeling his manhood twitch on my belly. My nerves were on edge, that tingling sensation every time he touched me, his actions to cause my arousal were incessant.

I heard him sigh and I felt sad.

He seemed exhausted I slowly stroked his hair, while my other hand stayed on his neck. His hands wrapped tightly around me and my legs on either side of his torso clenched a little.

We were in an obscene position and I couldn't help feeling nervous But I knew we wouldn't be disturbed. After all, he was the King.

"T-Tired? " I asked

Why did I stutter? Ahh was it because I could help but like it? I couldn't help but want his touch or touch him.

Did I seem lewd?

No...

I feel him grunt on my chest and I bite my lip as his chest pulsated over mine.

He takes in a deep breath, causing that hot breath to brush against my wet chest. I shudder feeling his lips over my neck. He pulled me up to get off him and I felt his length twitch against me again.

He stood up. Having no expression to his manhood erect right before and stepped out grabbed a cloth and dried his face and chest.

I was feeling much more dizzy.. The hot water, the alcohol. My hands rest over the edge of the tub and my head over them. My eyes closed assuming he was off to bed. I was very much sleepy. I knew once the King left, Maya or Lydia would surely just come to help me.

I was enjoying myself in the bath till I was lifted in his huge arms. My eyes snap open as all the water runs down from my body and makes his torso wet all over again.

He carried me to the bed. Sat me down and handed me a cloth. I take it. Staring at it and realised my brain wasn't working.

"You will catch a cold. "

I heard his angry voice when he snatched that cloth away from me and he froze with his eyes locked over my body.

I was confused. I frown till I realise was naked. Shrieking and covering myself in vain as he chuckled at me and covered my body with the cloth.

"Don't stay wet. You'll get sick"

I moaned inside as he licked my ear lobe and walked away.

I took my time drying my body. My legs touched the ground and I shivered at the freezing cold floor. Immediately ran back into bed and covered myself with the warm big blanket.

I closed my eyes for mere seconds before I felt the huge dip in bed and his arms circled around my body.

So warm.

He snuggled into me and He wouldn't let go. He wouldn't let me move and when I did move. He pulled my body to lay over his.

I couldn't remember anything after that. Only how his lips felt on mine before I drifted off to sleep.

‖ CHAPTER 22 ‖

"These are the servant's quarters. Your Majesty's ladies-in-waiting shall be here with, one of your choice living behind your chambers to attend to your needs at night. "

I nodded walking with Clara my eyes would occasionally brush past her huge sword as she walked with such grace with light armour on. Or most of the time with me in trousers and a coat like most men working in the castle.

She always carried her sword. She was assigned to be my guard, I suppose she must be very good at combat. I stare at the dark gardens surrounding the castles and courts wondering why the gardens before my chamber balcony were all filled with pretty flowers but the gardens near the court carried a dark look—void of flowers and greenery

"These were the back of the castle grounds. From here you can enter the court wing, The royals apart from the king and Queen reside here although many of them have left long ago and have their castles to the North of the kingdom. "

Following her through the open corridors I gave a light nod to her and smile looking around as we entered the other side.

I stare in awe at the huge architecture before me. The walls of the castle were grey and dark. But the design stood beautifully. In its own way.

"These are the halls that led towards the King's library. Yours will be on the other end."

I glanced at her before she escorted me towards my library.

She opened the doors and I was met with a huge room. The wall behind the huge desk was filled with books. And the dark walnut desk standing in the right middle of the two huge windows on either side of the room a bit further from the doors.

I trace my hand over the wood glancing at some papers and letters neatly placed over the table. Ink and pens with many other stamps placed over it.

I sigh.

"Why? I have no work. I am not to be involved in any court affairs. What's the use of such a beautiful room when I have nothing to do"

She seemed surprised at my words. She looked down before lifting her head. Her eyes stayed on the table.

"As the Queen you will be responsible for receiving any correspondence between the two kingdoms and reply with your current Kingdom's favour. You shall be responsible for all the castle servants. And holding informal meetings and balls for charity and political reasons"

I stared at her in awe as she spoke perfectly.

"The letters are from various merchants. And many other affairs that might need your approval. The papers, Sir Andrew will be explaining those."

I gulp nodding staring at the books.

"Well, Your Majesty. Shall we move on? "

I smiled.

"Call me Madam. That is fine. Yes, we shall" I answered looking around once before walking out with her.

She was very thorough with her explanation. She was stern, calm and strong. I liked her.

I smiled as she showed me around the cooking quarters.

As the cook served directly to the King and I, and bowed his head, I nodded eyeing that puff pastry behind him neatly stacked up together.

"I hope our dishes are to your liking Your Majesty."

He was a nice old man.... Yet, I was scared of him. He looked so soft and sweet, however, it was the aura around them that kept us at bay. I kept my head straight and walked past him while he kept his head bowed.

Taking the puff pastry from the plate and turning to leave through the doors.

I turned again one last time and smiled at the chuckling women behind him.

"Well then. Thank you for serving us. " I said before walking out with that puff pastry.

I smiled hearing some light laughter behind me. Clara looked at me and I smiled breaking the huge pastry in half and holding it out for her.

I see her eyes turn wide and she almost gasps.

"What? Take it. I can't eat all of this myself"

"N-no Madam we simply cannot. We only serve -"

"Eating a pastry I am sharing has nothing to do with serving me, Clara".

She slowly takes the other half and I smile walking ahead and eating it while I look around. She seemed to contemplate before I turned around to see her staring at me with that half-party in her hand, She immediately looked down and I saw a slight smile at the corner of her lip before I turned around.

She seemed very introverted. It was best I did not force her to act like my friend. It will take a while for her I suppose.

I never felt much worry or fear around women in this kingdom. Many walked past me, servants, maids. Members of the household and court. Even the royal family. Although some showed me their hostility towards me, I had a sense of calmness from the women. But the men scared me.

"This is the court. All the discussions regarding the Kingdom are carried out here. Although I cannot quite open the doors unless we are summoned by the King."

I nodded following her.

My eyes sparkled at the beautiful balcony we stood at. Right over my library. This was where intimate gatherings took place between the family and friends.

And on other days, it was just a greenhouse with beautiful couches and tables for tea.

"It is almost one, and you are scheduled to Lunch with His Grace's family. We should head back."

I sigh nodding.

The King didn't attend such lunches. So I sat at the head of the table with ten others. Two sisters of the King and three brothers. Close relatives who

I had not been introduced to yet. It was in my understanding that I had to pay my respects to them individually by this week.

I cleared my throat as they bowed to me before I nodded and sat down, "It is my pleasure meeting you all. Thank you for attending the Lunch." I said as Clara instructed me.

"No, it is our Pleasure." One of the elder sisters said and I smiled.

**

|| CHAPTER 23 ||

That lunch was quite, awkward. I could sense the disapproval from the elders except from the sisters of the king, I walked with a heavy heart to my chambers. I didn't quite understand why I was hated so much. It wasn't my choice to be in this position Nor did I ask for it.

As we walked past the courtroom with Clara behind me. I stare at the hallway leading to the King's library. I contemplate long enough before walking past it. I wanted to see him. I wanted to talk to him, perhaps because I felt attached to him. He gave me the warmth I wanted. He respected me, which I could see most of the court refusing to do. I can understand, I was the stranger in this Kingdom.

"Lydia, It's so tough, I rather be locked than face them."

"You will get through it madam I know it."

I was far too engrossed staring at the garden before, waiting for my tea, that I never noticed him enter the premises of that balcony. It was his faint presence that I sensed before I realized the king was right behind me. I froze still for a second as my heart gave one beat louder than others and my stomach flips reminding me of what he did to me last night.

Then this morning....

~

My embarrassed face had a tint of red as I woke up with a heavy head over his body. All naked, our skins touching. I could feel the light hair of his body on me as he held me tight. My hair was a mess of curls, my hand over his shoulder and my leg over his torso. I would burn if I slept anymore next to him. He was that warm.

When I opened my eyes I panicked trying to move away from him. I had to lift his heavy arms off my back and slowly sit up only for my body to give in and I fell back on the bed with my heavy head in pain. Then I heard him take a large breath before moving to sleep on his back. It only made me feel a flutter. When I kept staring his eyes opened. I felt my heart drop as I look away before he grabbed me and pinned me between his arms, his big head on my stomach and his hands wandering to my breasts.

"Y-Your Majesty -"

I cried out in that slight pain as he squeezed my right breast tight. So tight it hurt. He grunts, his mere voice sending me falling to the pit of a fall and my body shudders at his disapproval.

"X-Xerxes.." I correct myself and his hand loosens over me. I pout at my poor breasts being played with like some squishy toys. Yes, it felt good, yes I was wet like a pond. Yes, I found him very arousing when he did that. But my breasts were sensitive. Sore as a result of sleeping on them through the whole night and it hurt when he held them so roughly.

"Yes," That wasn't a question or just a mere response to me. That was the voice of approval. Even getting his attention was as dangerous as looking at the lion.

I shrieked as we heard a loud knock twice on those huge doors. He seemed amused at me as I jumped. I was embarrassed. There stood the butler waiting for his Majesty so he could be ready and here he was, naked, on me. Busy with something else.

I bite my lip as he bites me. I gasp pushing on his head but he didn't budge. Instead, my fingers curled in his hair and pulled them slightly feeling pain and pleasure as he continued his assault on my chest. When he finally pulled away, his lips suddenly curled up in an evil smirk.

I couldn't understand his amused expression while he stood up. His naked body glowed in the light sunlight peeking through the white curtains.

He ran his hand through his hair as I sat up pulling the sheets over me just enough to cover myself.

"Do not wander too far from this wing of the castle Ruby. Keep Clara close as possible. "

I stare into his eyes as his fingers lift up my jaw and I gulp nodding.

"Answer me, Ruby"

Oh... How I love hearing that from his lips.

"I will"

"Good girl"

My eyes fluttered when he kissed my cheek and left. That morning was filled with emotions. And I could help feel bubbly inside. Although my heart clenched a bit when he left.

And for the rest of the day, I spent with Clara. I felt at ease. Till now as I sat on the balcony. His footsteps came right behind me.

I dared to look behind me. And there he was standing in all his glory. I gulp standing up immediately and bowing slightly.

I see his eyes slowly fall down and then lift up my body as he walks towards me.

And suddenly, all the guards and my ladies-in-waiting were gone. Leaving us alone.

"Good afternoon your Majesty" I whispered not wanting to stay quiet and seem rude.

"You saw the castle grounds " He states lifting up my face with his fingers on my chin and I nodded.

"Good. You shall start your duties tomorrow. I'll have someone lend a hand if you wish. Any one of your choice"

I shook my head, "Anyone appointed by Your Majesty will be good enough"

He chuckled sitting on the couch before me. He sighs spreading his legs a bit more and then patting his left leg looking at me.

I bite my lip and look around before hesitantly sitting on his lap.

He kept his hands on the head of the couch and other on the end arm while I fidget with my dress staring down.

"How do they treat you. Your maids? "

"Very good"

"How is Clara? "

I glanced at him once before looking down, " Very stern and discipline. I like her. She seemed very strong"

" Glad to hear that. "

We hear the doors open and I immediately stand up to see Lydia and Maya carrying two trays of food and tea when his arm shoots up and grabs mine bringing me down back on his lap yet again.

I gasp as I jerk back into his arms but my butt lands on the couch and my legs over his thigh and hang between his legs.

He sighs in disappointment looking away as I feel that embarrassment washing over me again.

"What do I do with your Ruby"

He mutters as Lydia and Maya place the tray and serve us tea and biscuits .Me sitting with my hand on either sides of my body and my legs dangling on his.

While he threw his head back and closed his eyes.

I watch them leave and close the door before I sigh. Moving my legs off him slowly but his hand stops.

"You are gonna sit like this till I leave now"

Noooo....

I frown as his hand wraps around my waist while he leans in and takes his tea cup. Taking a sip and acting as if nothing happen.

While I sit there contemplating my life.

"I am sorry" I say as he keeps the tea cup back and leans back on the couch. His eyes definitely on me.

He says nothing. It just made me angry.

It wasn't my fault! I was sitting on his lap! He was the king! What would people think if they saw us like that!? And I know very well maids are. They are the sweetest women and best gossip ladys behind the big doors.

I pout staring at him as he had closed his eyes and leaned completely back on on the couch.

Pulling my lips in before I slowly lifted my legs off him. I knew he was awake. But he didn't do anything.

I gulp looking at the door and slowly pulling my dress up. When I placed my hand over his should he opened his eyes seeing me straddle him.

I clear my throat as his eyes open wide seeing me over his lap and my hands drop to his torso. So does my head.

"I am embarrassed of being intimate before them. I do not like gossip. "

I gasp feeling his hands on my bare skin. Inching up my thighs and stopping right at my bum. I shiver under his stare as he squeezed me.

"I don't think you are in a position to be embarrassed Ruby. Not when You are with me. And Not under my watch. "

I tilt my head to my side as his lips tickle my ear. His words hit my deepest core.

"You are my Queen. So let them see how you belong to me"

I moan as he kisses my neck and his one hand moves up from my waist to my chest. Pulling my neckline down and biting my chest yet again.

"No no.... We are outside... " I stutter and struggle to get my words out as he continues causing a havoc on my poor nerves by kissing every inch of me that was expose to him.

He stopped pulling up my neckline while my hands rest over his bicep. Watching him cover my cleavage and fixing my hair.

My heart fell as he looked into my eyes. My stomach clenched as he kiss me aofy before biting my lower lip. It made me cry out and pull away feeling the longing touch on his teeth on mine.

"I need to go."

He said pulling my hair to a side and kissing my neck. I almost grind on hais manhood feeling something pulsate down there.

He effortlessly stood up with me still on him and let's me down.

My dress falling to the sides and now a bit crumpled. I was straightening the dress. Avoiding his gaze. Already blushing like a cherry when he grabbed my jaw and forced me to look up to him.

"Don't wait on me for dinner. Yes?"

"Yes sir" Like an instinct I responded.

And he smirked pecking me, " Good girl. "

|| CHAPTER 24 ||

I smiled taking the letters from Andrew and he nodded once before leaving. I waited till the doors closed and slam the letter on the desk putting my hand on my head.

"How come I have to take care of the castle workers..." I mutter pouting opening the first letter and Fredrick sighs.

"I would advise hiring someone to take care of those however Your Majesty needs to see first for yourself the workings of the castle"

I narrow my eyes at Fred and snicker, "Sure. I have been told so many rules I can't keep up." I said reading the letter for permission of sending money for the guard's attire and signing over it for approval. Fred took the letter from my hand and noted the expenses as I instructed.

"Who was looking over these before?" I asked reading the next letter of an invitation for me to join the Tea Party for charity. I look over it intently before Fred spoke.

"The Eldest Daughter of the Late King, Your Majesty. She handed over her duties after your arrival."

"I see.."

She was quite the responsible sibling then.

"Could you please ask her to meet me then? Tomorrow for Lunch?"

"As you wish Madam."

I needed to be nice to at least one, the one who cared to be nice to me. Plus I would like to ask her about some invitations that I was in doubt about.

We heard a knock as I finished most of my work, "Enter"

"Your Majesty, the General, Sir Clark Vincent asks for your presence."

I closed the letter in my hand while glancing at Fred as he frowns glancing at me.

"I heard of no visits today."

"Yes, he apologises for his sudden arrival. He only wishes to have a few words regarding the lodges of the Soldiers coming back from the West. Since the King is not available it would be best Your Majesty looks upon this."

I stood up ready to receive him in the other section of my library where I could talk. But Fred turned to me.

"Perhaps I could go call for Sir Andrew and seek the King, SInce its the military matter..."

"It's about the soldier's Lodging for a few days, all I need is advice. I can arrange that. I don't think I should ask for help in every new situation Fred."

He seemed to be hesitant but nodded as I walked towards the doors.

"Yes, I shall receive him in the library itself."

The man nodded before leaving. Clara and Fred followed me behind, "I shall wait in the powder room."

I sigh sitting on the red chair and Clara bowed before leaving us.

"Why can't she stay?"

"Servants aren't allowed to stay for such meetings. I shall have to leave as well if Sir Vincent wishes."

I frown having no desire to be alone with a man. The room might be twice as big but for me standing with their kind becomes ten times smaller.

When the door opened, My heart sinks as I feel fear grip me. He looked terrifying. Long hair, a long beard, and sharp eyes and his face held a sickening emotion.

"Your majesty. It is a great pleasure meeting the new Queen, I hope you are well."

I gulp nodding and he takes my hand lightly kissing the back.

I wanted to snatch it away just as fast.

"How may I help you, General Vincent?"

He chuckled walking back and keeping his hand on the head of a couch before me. His eyes gave me a look that I dare not say.

"Nothing important of sorts, I only wanted to appear before our Queen a give my greetings. I have been guarding the forts of this kingdom for years and I see a new opportunity has raised. I could be of good help to you in certain ....situations."

I could feel the bridge between my eyebrows scrunches in confusion.

"I-I heard your soldiers will need an arrangement I shall have that done-"

"Ah.. Do not worry My Queen you do not need to involve yourself in such trifle matters. I shall have my servant arrange it."

How dare he cut me off?

My nerves were shaking under his gaze however I kept my eyes up to him. My head never lowered as I leaned back and my hands rest on the arms of the chair.

"Well then I hope you have a good day, Clark Vincent. I shall get back to my duties"

I heard a little snicker and he nodded and bowed.

My teeth clenched feeling as if he was making fun of me. I left that room having no further matters to discuss.

As the doors slammed shut behind me I picked up my dress and walked past Clara as she frowns at my angry expression.

"I do not want to see him again! "

I exclaim sitting on my couch and huffing.

"Did something happen Madam?"

I glance at her about to speak when Andrew speaks for me.

"How would you describe General Vincent? If I may ask"

Clara looked at him and paused.

"He asserts his authority in places he shouldn't. I hope that helps you understand his character more. "

Of course! He was the type of man who would do things beyond his authority on the bases of his victory.

I was never going to get used to being near them. I was disappointed at my fear.

~

That evening as I sat for my supper, I asked them to give it in my chambers. Sitting alone in the large dining room with multiple guards staring down just made me lose my appetite. I enjoyed the delicious food sitting by the fire and staring out at the windy sky.

"I heard Her Highness Katherine will be sending a painter for your portrait soon." Lydia said setting the bowl of fresh fruits before me and giving my finished plates to the servants. I dab my napkin over my lip looking at her.

"I didn't they do it here."

Lydia frowned as I sigh taking a sip of my water, "You think anyone would be proud to see me on the portraits of their Royal family?"

"I-I do not think you should say that Madam" Lydia said looking around to see if there were any maids around.

"It's true but." I leaned back on my chair and rang the bell.

The maids took the plates away as I undid my hair and walked to my powder room. Brushing my hair as Lydia helped me undress while Maya prepared a bath.

***

‖ CHAPTER 25 ‖

I sat in the warm water for quite a while. It was past midnight when I finished my supper. I was far too engrossed looking out the arch windows of the bathroom and submerging my body completely in the tub that as time passed by, I never realized I had been sitting there for an hour.

I heard the door of my chamber open and close, my eyebrow creasing at the sound. I had dismissed everyone as I wished to be left alone. Perhaps it was Maya, she always checked up on me before she slept. I liked her being so careful however sometimes I found myself asking for privacy. I had always done my own things with no one around me while I served as the Queen's lady-in-waiting.

Having maids around me only made me not want them.

"Maya is that you?"

I called out hearing no sounds for a while. I leaned forward peaking at the closed curtains of the room. When the opened I didn't expect to see him walk in naked.

I almost gasp seeing him, I thought I would be alone tonight. I figured he would walk straight to his chambers, tired and wanting sleep.

He said nothing, tossing his clothes aside from his hand and walking to the bathtub, I gulp as he sits in and leans back.

I didn't know why but he looked angry. His eyes stared at me making me nervous as I fidget with the washcloth.

"Come here."

I obey immediately. Scooting over right into his arms. He wrapped his hands around my waist pulling me over his body and guiding me to straddle him.

The silence continues as he rests his head on my chest, holding me tight as lets out a sigh.

It didn't look like he wanted to speak. So I stayed quiet, occasionally running my figures on his hair and neck.

He soon gets up with me in his arms. The water turned cold in the air dripping down our bodies as he took me out of the bath. He dried me before himself and tucked me into his chest closing his eyes.

I bite my lip wanting to say something. He looked tired, exhausted. Having no desire to disturb his already sleepy state I place a kiss on his cheek and tucked my head down in his chest. I felt him squeeze my waist from my back before getting comfortable.

~

"So you managed everything before me? Even the servants?"

The Eldest daughter, Regina nodded smiling. She was very elegant, poise, and quiet and only spoke about important matters. However ... Something about her didn't quite settle well. She seemed on the edge as she constantly looked up at me and then down. As if to stop herself from speaking.

"Would it be rude to ask for your help in some matters under my position ?"

I saw her eyes widen, sort of in a good way. She blinked and looked at her teacup.

"Would Your Majesty really need me for such matters?"

"Please, call me Ruby. And Yes, it is not an order, a request. Only if you wish."

I could see a small smile on her face and she nodded, "I-I would be happy to. I just, could I ask a favour before that?" She whispered leaning ahead as if to hide the glint of happiness from her maid.

"Absolutely."

"Would you keep this between us?"

I frown, nodding but hesitant. I was curious, I had been observing her for a while. She seemed very nervous. Her posture was confident, however, her speech said something else.

"May I ask why?"

She stayed silent, "No one can be involved in letters and papers addressed to the Queen, your Majesty."

Fred answered for her from behind me. I glance at him.

"But surely If I give you the authority-"

"No- It's not authority, I am ready to help Your Majesty if you need it however it would be best if it stayed between us. My uncle only gave me the work to fill in before you were crowned since I was educated enough."

I nodded with a deep frown. My eyes snap to her maid, she was waiting by the doors of my tea house. I sighed taking a sip of my tea.

"Regina, You are a part of the family. I would be happy if you were honest with me. And address me as your sister. If not a sister then perhaps an acquaintance."

She snapped her eyes at me and nodded slowly.

"Good, I would be waiting for you tomorrow. Now that this subject is over with. I would like to know more about you. If you do not mind..."

She frowned as I stood up.

"Let's have a walk."

I did feel intimidated by her. After all, she was one of them. Her beauty, I must say surpassed all the women I saw in the previous ball. I did not see her at the ball. Perhaps she was unwell. I dare say, she was the beauty of this kingdom. And I say it regarding elegance. Not just her face.

She had deep blue eyes, the ring around them dark brown. She seemed devoid of any touch. Pure. Her hair was black. Down to her lower waist. Her choice of clothing was simple.. Light colours of blush pink and cream. Her ears carried a simple pair of gold earrings and no more.

"I might be hated for what I am, here in your kingdom-"

She snapped her eyes at me and stopped walking.

I smiled looking back at her. Us in the middle of the Royal Gardens as our attendees stood far from us. Following us but at a distance.

"You might hate me for being a Queen. A position they call to be above all royals. I understand your people's disappointment."

"No-" I heard her whisper.

"I am aware of the court's decisions regarding my duties."

I must have caught her off guard.

Fredrick has filled me in about the court's certain distaste for me handling some affairs.

"I cannot back down since it would make me a coward but I can fight back cause it might lead to me being a rebel in a stranger's Kingdom.. I am much less stuck"

I said snapping a twig from the lower branch of a tree and trailing it along the road.

"No.... You are wrong your Majesty."

She stepped ahead and sat on the bench before me and smiled.

"I cannot speak for others but I and my sister Isla admire you. You are strong to entire this land, put up with his Majesty's behaviour. Put up with the behaviour of his subjects. It must be hard on you to leave your home...
"

Put up with him?

"No, I just got in the carriage and came here. I have done nothing. I do admit to having a fear for your kind. But I have met people who seem to get along well. I have judged you all.. "

She shook her head.

"I would be glad to help Your Majesty as long as you do not mention this to my Family-"

"Why? " I asked sitting down beside her.

She paused. Hesitated, with a deep frown over her head.

"They would not appreciate it. That's all. "

I asked no questions further. Nodding and agreeing to her.

"Why did you assume the King treats me badly? "

"I can only imagine what your fear must be. He has never been close to any of us since childhood. Even Mother feared him."

I frown.

"Feared? Why? "

"Well, it's the blood yes? It sends us all shivering cold. We cannot even look him in the eye. He has been ruthless to disobedient men and women of the court."

"I suppose he must have to put up his cold self for the better of the kingdom," I mutter

"He was cold before the crown and now he refuses to see eye to eye with his family as well."

"Oh.. "

"His Majesty will never change. We hope you never face his wrath-"

I smiled.

"No.. No, you do not understand. " She insists.

"I beg you to never go against his words. You never know what he might do. We know you are his mate.. However. We cannot say he would change his behaviour for this reason"

But... He has been so nice to me.

"I understand-"

I suppose it would be a bit weird to tell her how he was behind the doors. So I let her think as all others think.

There must be a reason the King held this act before us. He cannot show any vulnerability.

"Thank you for talking to me. I would love it if you brought your sisters here as well. Only if you wish. "

She nodded smiling.

As she bowed and left the gardens and narrowed my eyes at the maid leaning in to ask something. Regina seemed visibly annoyed at her.

"Fred, could you just dig around and see if I could trust her? Is there a way to do that? " I asked cutting some roses from the rose bush and handing it to Lydia.

"Yes of course. I'll let you know if anything is suspicious in two days. "

I nodded.

"Do you have the shawl I kept beside the bed with you? I feel cold inside the castle-"

"Yes. The sunlight doesn't reach the inner chambers, it just gets chilly very quickly-"

We both stopped on our heels as we saw Maya walk out from a room at the end of some other hall.

She almost seemed in shock as she saw me and Lydia. Immediately bowing and walking towards me.

"Madam."

I see a man walk out of the common room again and he froze for a second before bowing.

I held my laughter back as I nodded walking ahead and Maya following us.

"Well I didn't know you had a lover Maya"

I saw her blush as I glance at her.

"N-no your Majesty. We were just cleaning up -"

"Sure sure" I chuckle.

‖ CHAPTER 26 ‖

I was waiting for Regina in my study while writing down some things I had to get done when the doors opened and Andrew announced himself.

He looked like he was in a hurry. Bowing slightly before hurrying towards my table with long strides.

Fred stood up from his desk walking to stand before me as I frowned.

"Forgive me for intruding my Queen. There a question I have to ask."

I nodded looking up at him.

"Did Clark Vincent visit you within this week? "

"Yes-"

"What were the contents of your talk to him? "

I gulp glancing at Fred.

"Nothing specific. He had come to greet Her Majesty. We assumed he needed assistance settling his soldiers at the fort. Yet he never brought it up."

Andrew clenched his jaw staring at Fred as he explained.

"Was this sudden greeting planned? "

"No. It was not. I questioned the messenger however he said he had no authority to stop the General. "

Andrew nodded as Fredrick spoke for me. I licked my lip and gave a sigh looking away. I look back at Andrew as he seems occupied scrunching his eyebrows and looking down.

"Is this about how I broke the Royal protocol and gave him an audience? I heard I am not supposed to talk with any military personnel... Since. I am" I stopped right there.

"No-" Andrew immediately shuts me down.

"No, your Majesty. It is General Vincent who has no authority to ask for your audience. Forgive me for this sudden questioning. Have a good day. "

I frown as he bows and glances at Fred one more time before leaving.

I sigh leaning back on my chair.

"Well... What do we make out of this? "

Fred said nothing.

~

"Fred"

"Yes, Madam." I halt staring down at the training ground of the inner castle, The men fighting with such fierce force made me curious.

"Anything about Regina?"

"I have yet to confirm some things," I nodded slowly walking towards the training grounds as I saw a few of the soldiers who accompanied me here by carriage.

"The Blue Hall is this way," Fred states holding his hand out the opposite way and I nod. But stepped towards the training ground instead.

I was heading towards the hall when I saw the merchants. They had been called to present some of the new furniture designs. I had no desire to change much, but when I saw the north tower I felt the need to do something. It wasn't used for ages.

I heard from Maya, that it used to be a study room of Queen Persia. The King's grandmother.

I wished to refurbish it in her memory. I heard the King was close to his grandmother, I hoped this who help them understand my intentions of embracing their past.

"Madam, those the soldier's training grounds-"

"I am just curious..." I whispered looking at the open ground and stepping down. They didn't notice me yet.

Fred looked around and before he could see me I had entered the ground looking around at the huge men. They were scary.

"Watch out!"

Before I knew it I saw a spear flying towards me. I didn't gasp, froze to the ground as my heart stopped. The spear stopped mere inches from my head.

I gulp looking beside me.

Fred grounds the spear on the grass before moving away from me.

The ground suddenly turned silent and I realized how stupid I was. I had stopped their training and now they had to let go of their swords and weapons to bow to me.

"It was me. May your Majesty show me mercy. We never expected your visit and I was reckless."

A young soldier stepped ahead from the crowd and got on his knees making me gulp and press my back to the cold wall behind me. He hung his head low waiting for my decision as if I would do something.

Fred stood silent as I judged myself and them. Where are they making fun of me?

Could they believe I was able to do anything to them? Me before these hundred beasts.

"For-"

The Queen never apologises to her servant Ruby...She can only acknowledge.

"No fret, I came here to see the training grounds," I replied taking back the previous words.

He nodded I could suddenly see his body tremble as he kept his eyes on the ground. Sweat dripping down his temple and I frown.

"You can go back to your training," I said looking at everyone. Fear in my stomach but confidence in my voice. They bowed once more before stepping back but never picked up their swords. He on the other hand stayed as he was.

"It was addressed to you too ... what's your name?" I asked

"Oliver your Majesty. I await my punishment." He says.

I blink at him and glance at Fred. Fred stood with no expression on his face.

"There is no need to wait for it. I asked you to go back to your training.-"I pause as he gulps, I learn just a little seeing his hands tremble.

"Believe me, this isn't the first time I have had a weapon come at me." I softly said before turning around and smirking slightly.

"Punishment is necessary for them."

Chills filled my spine as I heard Clark Vincent's voice. I see Fred look behind me and bow. I looked back to see the soldiers at guard and Oliver on the ground still. As Vincent strides towards him from the very back. My teeth clenched and my hands turn to fists.

Why was he here? I thought he left for his fort.

His voice was nothing compared to the fear he gave me with his presence. Not like Xerxes. This fear of doing something evil to others. He looked like a diabolic man. This fear was like anger. Just settling at the pit of my stomach as I anticipated for him to do something bad.

"General Vincent. I was told you left for the fort-"

He cut me off, daring me to speak over him. His presence was shocking, and it turned my fear into anger when he cut me off.

"I was dealing with a few crooks and cranes back here. I didn't think I would have the pleasure of seeing your majesty. At a training ground full of our men.."

That was a suspicious comment that I kept at the back of my mind.

"And a man who committed such an unlawful act should be punished."

I clenched my jaw glancing at the soldier. My body filled with anger as he took his sword and put it over Oliver's neck.

"He deserves death for attempting to harm the Queen."

I could see his body tremble but he stayed quiet.

I take a deep breath before turning to the general, "You plan on killing him ?"

He looked at me and smiled, "This is what we do here. No mercy is shown to traitors."

"I applaud your punishment general Vincent. Mercy only shows weakness. But, this particular traitor has been under my wing for quite a while now, and I do not like decisions made for me. "

I was trembling underneath. I didn't even know if I was allowed to take a soldier serving the King under my wing. But this man had to know I do not give up without a fight.

"Which is exactly why I have to make an example of him. No one shall harm you then-"

"I command you to withdraw your sword, Clark Vincent," I state as he suddenly freezes.

IMP NOTE :

The book will have slow updates however if you wish to read further 20 chapters they are uploaded on Dreame under my primary Profile [CRAZYWOLF189]

Thankyou for supporting me!

|| CHAPTER 27 ||

H is hand slowly moved back and his head hung low.

"Oliver, stand up and get back to your training. You shall report back to me once you are done. Well then General I hope you have a good stay at the castle before you leave. Now excuse us."

I said so in haste before turning around only to jounce into a chest.

My breath hitched, drying my throat, his presence which I had not noticed suddenly filled the air turning my body still as a rock.

My body melts as his hand wraps around my back preventing me from jerking back before he lets go.

I realise how I disrupted a training ground, possibly went against some rules and took a soldier under my staff. Such unprofessional behaviour was surely embarrassing not to mention the fear that set inside me as The King let go of me as looked behind.

When I lifted my eyes, all I could see was a neutral expression.

"My King." Clark Vincent gets on his knees and bows as all the others do.

I frown stepping back and behind him.

My eyes glance at Fred who never looked up to me.

"You have to decency to be on your knees for your king. Have you forgotten the protocol for the Queen?" Andrew's voice booms through the arena and I flinch as the king touches his sword.

Vincent said nothing.

"Who threw it?" Andrew asked Fred staring at the spear.

"It was me, My King," Oliver speaks up, Still on the ground.

I rolled my eyes, Great. Now I have to explain everything all over again.

"Leave him be," I whispered to The king softly.

I know he heard it although he had no response. His other hand touched mine only slightly, for a minute before he lifted his legs and bumped it into Oliver's leg.

I found it inhumane but again, they weren't humans.

"Back to work." The King said softly looking around but his command didn't need to be loud or harsh. Just three words were enough.

"General Vincent. There are some matters I would like to discuss. Please wait in the common library in the east wing." Andrew said.

I saw him trying to look up but he couldn't.

I realised none of them spoke before the King. I realize none of them ever even looked at him. I hide my face like a coward as everyone stands up and backs away, The king turns to me as a result my heart picks its pace, scaring me of his next remarks. I feared for my life knowing I did something wrong.

He said nothing to me, only glanced and moved ahead walking towards the halls of an unknown building. Andrew steps towards me as Fred finally lifts his head.

"He shall see you for dinner. Please come to the grand balcony by eight."

"Andrew!" I called and he immediately turned to me with a worried look.

I didn't know why but he was so much like the king. In a good way.

"Are they going to punish Oliver. ?"

"The decision is yours, My Queen. Not of ours to make. Have a good day." He said nodding at Fredrick once before leaving.

I sighed shaking my head and walking back up the stairs and heading towards the Blue Halls passageway.

***

I was yawning walking the halls, ready to have my evening tea, but the weather had turned warm and I wished to go take a walk in the castle gardens first.

"Maya could you-" I stopped looking back and only saw Lydia.

I frown. What's she supposed to attend to me today?

"Didn't I give you a day to yourself Lydia?"

She purses her lips, "Maya felt indisposed today. So I am in her place Madam."

"Oh"

Well, that's no problem.

I had nothing to do the whole day after my work. I wonder if this was how a queen's life is. Just work and sleep. Perhaps I could do something to entertain myself?

I had no desire to host any parties unless they were important, and I could never expect to spend time with the King as well. He seemed far too busy.

"Madam, Princess Regina is here to see you."

I smile looking back as she bows before walking towards me. Her maid is on her heels to catch up to her but I halt her.

"We will take a walk, wait here." Lydian nodded waiting with her maid as I gestured for Regina to follow me.

"Forgive me for intruding on your alone time-"

"No, Please. If anything I feel bored."

She smiled softly before speaking, "I have finished replying to many of your messages from the court addressing the issues at the border. I was here to take your advice and seek for approval on send aid to the farms out at the eastern borders. I have it written on paper and wondering if Your Majesty would allow some of the funds to be given for these aids."

I look at the paper in her hands and take it. Reading the required people and resources for helping the people and smile.

"Yes, of course, I would allow it. I shall have it signed by today and have someone look over it so it goes smoothly."

She sighs nodding.

"Next week, you are to keep an informal ball for charity. For the people working in mines. All that's collected will be kept in your treasury before it goes to them."

I nodded.

"Under whose guidance does this charity run?"

"Madam Sofiya, the dutchess. She has been running charities for miners for ages."

"I see. Then will you invite her as a guest for the upcoming tea party I so have to arrange?"

Regina nodded.

"How is your work? Is it too much burden? Shall I appoint someone for help?"

Regina shook her head.

"No, Madamn Thankyou. But I love working."

I could never quite ignore her shy frightened face whenever she talked about work.

"Why do you seem so -scared of your family knowing you work?" I asked frankly.

"No, I-I don't know."

She was much hesitant so I only nodded and spoke no further on her issue.

‖CHAPTER 28‖

"Your Majesty"

We both looked behind to see Fredrick and Oliver standing before us. They bowed before Oliver kneeled on the ground taking me by surprise.

"Your majesty I am at your humble service! "

I gulp glancing at Regina who was staring at me. We frown and I blink unable to decide my words in reply.

"Um." I clear my throat.

"Oliver. What brings you here? "

"Who is he? " Regina softly whispers.

I glance at her but Fredrick answers for me.

"He is your Majesty's second guard. Since I am unable to attend to you all day I believe Oliver can stay by your side and help if needed. "

I give Fred a weird look before walking to him.

"Why isn't he where he is supposed to be? With the Knights? "

Fred looked at me and lowered her gaze again.

"Madam. I believe you took him under his wing after the unfortunate incident at the training grounds. He would be beheaded if you dispose of him. Therefore do as you wish. "My mouth almost hung open but I knew better than to show such embarrassing emotions.

"I-"

I didn't know he would be sent to me.

"Well. Uh. Sure." I look at Regina as she stands there in confusion.

I already had Fredrick as my messenger and Clara as my guard. Plus Maya or Lydia always followed me with them.

It would be such a trouble having so many around me while I carried my basic routines.

I hesitate but finally decide to hand him over to Her Highness.

I look at Oliver and smile as I gesture to him to raise.

"You will be stationed at my library with Princess Regina. You will be her primary messenger and guard".

" Madam! " I heard Regina's soft voice.

"Madam he is your guard"

"I am appointing him as yours. Well then. That's settled. Oliver, I hope Fredrick has shown you to your quarters. And your roles will be explained in detail tomorrow.. "

He bowed and they left us alone.

"I-I do not think my uncle would like me having a guard"

I frown, " You are a princess. Of course, you need one.".

She dropped her head nodding.

"There is no need to worry. You can always tell him I was the one to make such decisions."

She nodded again with a faint smile. I couldn't understand why she looked so scared. I had to get to the bottom of this.

***

I take my hair pins off placing them over the desk as Maya enters my chambers.

"Are you alright? " I ask.

"Yes, Madam. I was unwell. Forgive me. "

I nodded keeping my earrings in Lydia's hand. I noticed Maya's fidgety behaviour but chose to ignore it.

Wearing a simple gown and having my hair down but only a few strands pinned up I made my way to the dining room for supper.

As always it was empty with only the 4 guards stationed at the doors. I sigh sitting down.. Extremely hungry.

I was busy having the soup when I heard the doors barge open. I almost dropped my spoon seeing the King.

I could quite literally sense his anger. My eyes subtly glance at the guard who gulped standing still.

I stood up. My hands press on the tabletop and I look at him.

He was soaked in rain outside as he dropped his coat kept his sword over the table and took off his light armour tossing it on the ground.

I could feel my body tremble as he walked straight to me. His eyes deepen as I stare at them. Water dripped his hair to his neck. His skin was shining under the candlelights above us.

His lips were apart as if he were about to speak while his hands were in fists.

I wish I could deny it. But I am a sinner. I liked it, I liked my fear towards this man. I liked how the king had me on my last nerves ready to run away. Because somewhere in my body I felt butterflies.

I knew he wouldn't hurt me. But that feeling of almost seeing him in anger ready to grab me and take me was much unexpected.

His face was rigid today as he closed our distance and pulled me into his cold body kissing me.

Shocked. I stood still. My hands pressed over his chest as he roughly kissed my lips his hands gripping my waist and others on the back of my head.

I couldn't keep up. Whimpering at the pain of his teeth against my lower lip.

I pulled away to catch a breath and my head hung low while he pushed my head ahead to lean on his chest and kissed my head.

I didn't know what to say. I was too engrossed in the feeling of his hand over my waist. The soft fabric let his hand feel my curves and feel his warmth although he was soaked.

"S-supper? "

I asked.

"Hmm," That was all he answered kissing my neck and making me bite my lip hard to hold my moan. I wanted to get away from him just to take a breath. Because he left me breathless, hot and wet before sitting on the chair beside me.

"Serve" His voice booms through the area as the maids scramble to serve him.

His hand casually over my back resting on the head of my chair, while his other rubbed a tower over his wet hair, as the butler slowly served him and put a plate of cream stew before me.

I bite my lip at the silence as he eats his plate while the butler serves him wine. I shook my head when he offered me some. I had to wake up tomorrow with a fresh head to get some things done.

"You have appointed Oliver as your guard?"

His voice touches my ear and I almost jerk away realizing how close he was. I didn't even notice him lean into me. Turning my head to him, our lips almost touching I shook my head.

"I-I do not need so many guards. Having Fredrick and Clara follow me everywhere is overwhelming enough, so I stationed him in my library. Where Lady Regina works."

My heart sank after I realized I had taken her name. She had specifically told me not to tell anyone and what if the King was against it?

I gulp looking at him waiting for his reaction but he was busy eating.

"D-Do you mind her working with me?" I asked

I had no desire to approach this subject. But It was better I talked about it before he did something.

"No."

A simple 'No' followed.

I frowned. If the king had no objections against her, why would she be so anxious about it? Surely the family wouldn't care if the King did not right?

Before I knew it, I sat before the fire warming my feet when I felt him stand behind me. My heart stopped as his lips softly touched my neck. I couldn't help but close my eyes and love it

.

|| Chapter 29 ||

Heat inundated my body as he picked me up and tossed me on the bed softly. My nightgown was thin and sheer, so my skin could feel his hands over me even before he touched it.

I let out a shaky breath watching him undo his trousers and pull his shirt over his head throwing it on the floor. I lay there, my hands beside my shoulder. In fist and my legs closed together.

I shivered, but not cause of the cold.

When he kept his knee on the bed, coming towards me. I felt something hurt in my bud. It was clenched tight as he crawled towards me. His hand caressed my waist while I gulped and bit my lip.

I covered my mouth to hold back the scream as he flipped me over suddenly and a loud smack echoed through the walls.

My bum had a sting on it.

I couldn't realize fast enough as another slap echoed and I whimpered softly feeling my wetness pooling around my bud I couldn't believe how I could like being slapped.

I gasped as his hand wrapped around my neck, the way his fingers wrapped around the front of my neck and pulled my head up, I felt my body melt and freeze again like a pool of ice. His body was over mine while his other hand grabbed my wrist holding me down on the bed.

"What were you doing on the training grounds? "

His voice was threatening me to speak, anything of his disapproval and I would be punished.

"I " I could hardly speak. My tongue was tied between his touch and my flimsy mind.

"I was walking through the halls and wished to take a-a-look..." I gasp feeling his manhood press against my bum.

"A look at a what my dear?"

My eyes shut and almost roll back as he softly grinds himself over me. He was teasing me. And I was falling for it.

"I asked you a question" he grunts pulling my neck up causing me to whimper under him.

I could feel his breath over my neck. Every time he breathed out it tickled my skin causing my nerves great pleasure. I had chills in my arms.

"I.." my mouth couldn't hold it in. As I let out a soft moan with his grind.

My eyes never opened but I felt his hand move my hair aside and his lips pressed against the back of my neck. Hot and wet.

"You failed to answer a simple question?"

I whimper as I feel him move and another slap echoes through the room. My bum is not hot and in pain.

"F-Forgive me-"

"What was Clark speaking to you about?"

I gulp as he pulled me back on my back. My teeth scrapped against my lower lip holding back the pain on my bum.

I gasped as he pulled me up and ripped my laces.

"Let me make it clear to you my queen. I do not care who you talk to. But I will not allow men to initiate a conversation with you."

The cold wind hit my now bare body as he ripped my nightgown in half with ease. I was bare. Exposed and all his to see.

His hands effortlessly wrapped around my waist pulling me closer and kissing my neck almost biting me.

I gulp, ready to talk and hold back the feeling of sudden pleasure that entered me.

"I wanted to see the training grounds."

I whispered and he halted his attention to my bare neck. Leaning back only a few inches to look at me. His eyes held such pressure that I could hardly open my mouth. All I could do was tremble.

"When I approached them unannounced. An arrow flew past me. General Vincent approached me and had his sword by Oliver's neck."

I feel him staring down at me. My eyelids flicker and I continue, " Forgive me. I shouldn't have-"

He tilts my chin up, "I do not want to talk to him. He has no authority. Understand? You send Fredrick straight to inform me if anyone here tries to have an audience with you. Do you understand Ruby?"

I only nodded.

I thought nothing of it. It was better I was never allowed to have any interactions. I can hardly understand their traditions let alone their court.

"yes-" the rest of my words were shaky and inaudible. When his lips attached to my neck and followed down to my stomach.

His hands ran across my body making me shiver. My hands stay on the bed. Waiting for a moment to touch him. But my brain was foggy. I couldn't bring myself to say or think anything. I was busy, busy feeling what he did to me.

My throat choked as he settled himself between my legs and I gasped feeling him right there, I almost clenched it.

My screams were soft and filled with pleasure as he kissed me roughly before his hands did their best to grab all of my breasts and squeeze them as hard as possible. As I lay whimpering under him. He was content biting my nipples and pulling on them through his teeth.

"Wait no!" I could hardly get it out of my mouth as he let go of my breast from between his teeth and looked at me.

When I looked at him I couldn't quite describe his face to myself. His eyebrows tilted inwards. His eyes looked at me and his face held a softer look. He never looked soft, just soft enough to not look angry.

And his hands suddenly massage me while his finger rubs over my nipple where he just bit me.

"You don't talk much. Why"

I gulp.

How can I when you pull my attention to what you are doing to me?

I look at him in my wilting state. I want him to stop yet..keep going.

His hand travels down my chest to my waist. Squeezing it once makes me feel embarrassed of not having a completely flat stomach. I gulp as he keeps going down. My fingers snap to dig in his arm as he pushes his finger inside me.

His eyes stay right on me as I cry out in pain.

"I-It hurts-" I whimper closing my eyes utterly embarrassed and having no knowledge of what to do.

"I know baby"

My heart swelled up. I heard him say that and I felt myself melt like a puddle.

His voice was so smooth. Yet manly. Never had I quite felt like cowering in the corner but letting him engulf me at the same time.

A sudden cry brought me back as I felt a sharp pain. Then his finger slid inside me.

I shut my eyes digging my fingers into his arms without conscience.

My head tucked into his arm as my back arched letting him slide it in further. I gasp feeling the pleasure burst inside as he slowly continues.

~*~

"I want to"

She said as he stared at her. His eyes took on all her body in. Her beautiful legs were over the soft sheets of her bed. Her bed was like feathers. Her pillows were much softer than his.

He always found himself amused by how she blushed with the slightest of gaze. Her cheeks would paint red and her chest would get hotter, and as she breathed, they would swell up and almost perk up her nipples.

Her white hair sprawled so perfectly over her shoulder and fell down her waist. The curls at the ends of her hair made him chuckle in his head. He would always find her fussing with them.

Her hands were so soft. Too clean to be touched.

When he heard her words he was ecstatic. His wolf wanted to ravish her body. Do whatever it took to have her moan in his ear. But the love in him hesitated.

Would she be okay? Would his mate be in pain?

But he couldn't hold himself back even if he wished.

She was very beautiful.

He wanted to mark every inch of her body. Have the people see who she belonged to. He laughed at his thoughts sometimes, they would never dare even if they could...she would never get a single cut on her body.

She was untouchable to them.

He crept up the bed kissing her thighs lightly before pressing his tongue softly over her bud. She gasped at that newfound feeling of his lips between her legs. Something she didn't know felt so good and different, he softly inched closer, kissing her stomach before playing with her breasts. He loved her breasts, They were extremely soft. handful and he loved how they jiggled every time she moved under him.

"I will not stop once I start Ruby. You have to understand that."

|| Chapter 30 ||

His words were nothing but ingenious and stern.

She gave him a look of worry and fear as he kissed her lips.

"I cannot stop once I claim you like this, I need you to know how much of a beast I can be."

He knew his strength, He wasn't a virgin like his pure mate. He had taken many women. But they weren't human like her. And they would be left immobile for hours after it. He liked rough, he liked to do things that would bring his mate pure fear.

He wasn't soft, even thou he tried. He wanted so badly to tie her up and taste every single part of her body. Play with her and give her the sort of pleasure and pain no woman could get in bed.

Xerxes loved hearing her whimper and moan. He loved the soft voices she gave as he teased her. Something she would never show another man in this world. He had that. She gave him the embarrassed yet aroused look no other man could see. Her body was only for his eyes. It gave him immense pleasure knowing she was only his. And she wanted him.

Xerxes often found himself hating humans because they fear them naturally. He feared if she didn't like him touching her. What if she left him?
Not that she could, but what if she didn't like him?

Hearing those words from her mouth gave him such happiness.

She wanted him to claim her. And now he was worried if she could take in
his rough ways.

Ruby cried as he softly entered her. Her cries made him hate himself. All
he could do was kiss her all he could to make her feel better.

"I cannot do it if you keep crying like that...It makes me angry."

She whimpered holding back her cries. But as she stopped and took the
pain silently, Xerxes changed his mind.

"On the contrary, I changed my mind. Scream as much as you wish baby. I
want to hear your voice. I like it...very much."

With that, he pushed inside her making her scream. He could feel something wet spread across his cock and he knew it was blood. But he didn't
stop.

She screamed again as he did it over and over until the cries of pain turned
into whimpers and moans.

She was trying her best not to dig her nails harder in his arms. But he was
already left with many scratches.

And when she started liking it, he stopped for a brief second to see her react.
She looked at him with her tearful eyes and begged through them. Asking
him why he stopped.

"Xerxes-"

"Beg"

His aura changed so quickly. It was an order. His eyes had turned neutral as he softly wrapped his fingers around her neck. His other hand was beside her head and he leaned closer.

"Beg for me, Ruby."

"Please.." her fragile voice said as he continued.

But he didn't last long as her voice was far more arousing to him than he thought. She moaned as he kept going till he suddenly pulled out making her wince in pain.

She felt something warm spread over her stomach as he took in shallow breaths.

She couldn't move, and the pain between her legs suddenly took over, as she lay, closing her eyes unable to speak. She was exhausted and in pain but she was happy. He had taken her when she consented. He listened, and he didn't force her like she thought. She felt herself falling asleep soon after.

But for him, it was panic. Before he could even think of lying down, his eyes had seen the blood. His heart suddenly beat fast as he cleaned her with the thin sheet and cupped her cheeks.

"Ruby?"

She wasn't responding. He clenched his jaw picking her up and taking her straight to the bathtub. As he sat her in and pushed away her hair he noticed his mark, he hadn't even realized how many marks he had given her. Her chest, neck, breasts were covered in them.

Cursing under his breath he cleaned her up and took her to the couch. The sheets were covered in drops of blood and he was scared he had hurt her for good.

Xerxes had never felt such panic before. And he knew the consequences of having a mate now. She could become his greatest weakness and he could crumble under it soon enough.

He forced her to have water slowly as he held her before the fire wrapped her up in a new blanket and snuggled up in his arms.

She was content, but him. He had something new to worry about.

***

[Ruby]

When I woke up, I found myself sleeping over his body. The fire lit up the room just enough, as I pushed my head off his chest slightly. But even such a small movement had him opening his eyes and tightening his arms around me.

His eyes were dull. Like he had been awake for some time.

"How do you feel? Are you still in pain?" he asked sitting up with me still in his arms. The blanket over me fell exposing my bare body to the air. But it was warm because of the fire.

The slight sting between my legs continued to remind me of what we had done just a while ago. I was embarrassed to look at him.

It was what married people do. I was after all his wife. But it felt so...weird. I was feeling shy. Embarrassed that he had seen my everything and now we had done what I only heard from my maid once.

I gulp nodding. My body was sore.

I gasped feeling his hand slide down my waist and between my legs. I held his wrist and tried to stop him.

I was too sore. I couldn't take it again.

"No.Your majesty it hurts.."

But his fingers placed upon me and I wince slightly digging my nails into his arms again.

I felt his finger touch me and he pulled away. My eyes stared wide at him in utter embarrassment as he looked at his finger.

What is he doing...

"You aren't bleeding still. That's good. I will ask the maids to take a look at you later." he said cupping my face with both his hands and kissing my forehead.

Being in his arms made me feel at ease. Suddenly I didn't wanna part with him. He pulled the blanket over my shoulder and stood up. His body is bare like me. I couldn't help but grab his arm lightly.

He froze looking back.

"Are you leaving?" I asked.

"No, but I can't have my wife still naked as the maids come clean the bed. "

I felt like my cheeks heated up as he left. I heard him ring the bell after he put his trousers on and helped me into my nightgown.

I couldn't find the words to describe how I felt.

I was nervous. What if he didn't like it? And...the maids. They would know what happened just now. I knew I bled. And it was very embarrassing.

Just the thought that people would know what we did made me curl up in the corner.

***

"Send these to Lady Regina. Have her look over them before approving them" Fred bowed before taking the letters and leaving my study room.

I sigh looking at the now empty table and wonder if I should take a hobby perhaps.

My thoughts were interrupted by the doors slamming open. I almost flinch but my heart swells up and beats faster as I see him walking through the door.

"Out"

His command send Clara and Andrew out the door in seconds. As the doors closed, I could feel my stomach turning as he walked towards me in his dressed-up suit and his sword by his side.

He held that same expression. It never changed unless he was with me at night.

Cupping my face and laying his lips over mine his majesty pulled me closer and trapped me in my chair.

"I am leaving for a meeting. I shall be late. Don't wait for me. Yes?"

His voice was always so demanding.

"yes"

He nodded pulling away. I stood up as he looked out the windows of my balcony.

"There will be 3 guards stationed outside your chambers. You have to tell them who you could let in before you sleep. "

Again? He was adding more and more guards around me every second.

"but-"

"I have already made the decision. You may take Fredrick, Clara and any one of those guards with you if you wish to leave the castle. I cannot have anyone lay a finger on you." he whispered cupping my cheek with his hand and kissing me.

I hardly think anyone can come closer to me because of him.

But I nodded in hesitation to satisfy him. I didn't want him to be angry.

After that week...as I continued my work....my mind would wander to what happened the night before.

Ever since we did it the first time. The king didn't spare me. He would find every reason to touch me.

There wasn't a night we didn't sleep bare in those sheets after that.

He would rip my gowns off and forbade me from wearing them when he was sleeping next to me.

After that week he left the castle for a few days regarding some investigations.

I suddenly realized how I had started to feel empty without him around.

‖ Chapter 31 ‖

"S" hall I call for something warm, Madam? Perhaps ginger tea?"

I looked at Lady Regina but she shook her head.

"Are you unwell?" I asked

She had become much more comfortable around me as we spent more time during dusk. I would often invite her to my garden for tea and we would read the books we preferred in silence.

"No Madam, I am well." She said pressing her kerchief to her mouth.

I ran my eyes down her temple to her cheeks. Lady Regina was quite the beauty herself. She had dark hair, her skin reminded me of honey as it shined under the sunlight with a golden tint. Her eyes were big and beautiful. I wondered why such a beauty of the castle carried herself with isolation and gave the perception of a brooder. I didn't wish to pry in her personal life. But I was worried after my eyes settled on her visibly wounded hands.

"Your hands.."

She was startled as I grabbed her palms and found marks on her wrists. She immediately retreats her hand covering them back with her sleeves My obvious questioning stare moved to her maid but she was already looking at her mistress as concerned as me.

"Who did this?" I could feel my anger rising.

I knew she was weak, I had heard from the place maids how she was but a fragile girl put under immense pressure by the kingdom. She has a weak body, so seeing a wound on the Eldest princess in the kingdom was a shock to me.

"I-I had a minor accident.-"

I didn't believe her. I knew those types of wounds. I had seen it on many soldiers.

When your hands are in shackles, or held so hard they create deep impressions.

"Lady Regina. This isn't a wound you get by accident. " I spoke turning my body towards her but I noticed Fred standing some steps away from us. Our eyes met, possibly giving him an insight to my worries as he nodded slightly and walked away.

I might have spoken out of turn. It was none of my business. Yet, I couldn't find the strength to stop.

This time I glance back at her maid.

"Have you not been attending to your mistress?" I ask politely.

I tried to hide my anger but in vain.

The maid, startled at my question immediately responded by bowing her head.

"No, Your Majesty. I am always..."

"Madam. She isn't at fault. I am just clumsy-"

"She must attend to your needs as frivolous they might be. "

" I understand. I shall be careful."

I sat in silence. I knew she wasn't truthful. But I would only make her hate it if I pry any further. Instead I took her to garden of herbs. Perhaps she might feel better having the scent of fresh herbs around.

I smiled as she smelled the lavender.

"I plan on harvesting these and giving them to place maids. They are growing incessantly."

She laughed.

"Ever since Your Majesty asked these to be planted they have brought some grace into the inside gardens," Lydia said cutting some off and putting them in a basket before handing them to the princess's maid.

"I will be harvesting my herbs soon too. Feel free to come to get them whenever you like." she nodded smiling.

It was the day after when I sat across my garden writing a letter to my mother when I noticed Fred walk in.

"Leave us," I said and the two maids behind me left except Lydia.

He bowed his greetings before showing me a disappointed face.

"My reports say perhaps, Lady Regina is being suppressed by General Vincent. He has access to the personal chambers of their family. It is also confirmed he was and currently is an advisor for the King's mother and his Highness Raphael, His Majesty's younger brother. It seems that she has been forbidden from being involved in court affairs. And General Vincent planned on marrying her to his son but the engagement was halted due to your coronation."

My head suddenly starts fitting in the loose puzzles.

"Is...is there any sign of...abuse?" I asked softly running the top of my finger over my tea cup rim.

I was hoping for a no.

His silence gave it away.

"General Vincent is a tyrant as they all call him. He likes the power he has. I wouldn't dare speculate." he paused.

Such a political answer.

"You amaze me with your neutral answers Fred."

"I dare not accuse before confirming" He said with his head hung low.

I nodded.

There was silence as I sighed leaning in my chair and rubbing my temple in frustration. I tried to get some water before Fred stepped in to pour some for me.

"Should I inform The King's men"

I looked up and shook my head," I do not know whether I can involve myself in this matter,Fred."

He only nodded and stepped back before haulting his step and looking at the garden gates.

"Oliver" I acknowledged his bow as he walked towards me and kneels before me.

"What is it?"

"I wish to report something to your highness"

Since there was no one but Fred and Lydia beside me I sit up in my chair and nod.

He stayed kneeled with his head down. I saw him blink before he lifts up his gaze.

"I have been observing Lady Regina these past days under Sir Frederick's command. General Clark seeks her audience quite often. In their personal library. He has been persuading the Lady to marry. And his tone is...much lower than respectful. "

My eyebrows creased. I felt my heart drop as I heard that.

"He slapped her. "

My eyes immediately met Fredrick.

"You witnessed it?" Fred spoke out with a strict tone but Oliver's stern nod indeed confirmed what I feared.

"On what basis does these conversations usually go on? "

Or... The abuse. May I say.

"I assume he forbade the Lady from involving herself in any court affirs. He seems displeased. He asked her to resign her post and marry within the end of next month."

"Was there anyone else present-" Fred's question was answered swiftly. .

"Yes sir."

I was utterly disturbed by that news. I made haste towards the dining hall as the King waited for me. As my heart fluttered at the thought of being next to him. My stomach however felt guilty of knowing Lady Regina's condition yet having no proof to present this situation to the King.

I suppose there would be much rebelling if I were just go upto him and say General Clark was a hateful of a man.

We had nothing to help her unless. She herself admitted to it. Or... The person who was with them. And I knew no one would speak up for the princess.

***

‖Chapter 32‖

"I used to love swings. And sitting at the banks of frozen lakes. When I was ten. Last time I did it. I was sixteen. Just starting my studies. "

"What made you stop."

Even his voice made my core move. It was so gentle yet husky. It kept me on my edge. Something I found enduring. While his voice held me in my stance, his fingers dragged across my back giving me occasional shivers. And when they would stop to wrap around my waist, I would bite my lip hoping to hold my tongue from giving up any voice of embarrassing pleasure.

I could never have imagined, me talking about my childhood to a man who seemed the least interested in anything but his kingdom and wars.

But here he sat, behind me staring into my soul and listening to my incessant talks. When I would stop he would ask me more. But when I asked, I would get a curt reply. It discouraged me from asking deep questions about his life. Instead, I stuck with asking jolly ones.

For example, how he used to love pears until he saw a bug in it and never touched a pear again. It was amusing.

"Why did you stop? ".

My eyes shut close immediately as his lips touched my shoulder. His fingers opened my laces in no time. The sleeves of my gown dropped below my waist exposing my bare back to him.

I gasped out loud as he grabbed my upper arm and held me in place as he bit my lower back. Sucking on my skin and marking it like the rest of my body.

I couldn't speak when he did that. I just sat there in shock soaking the pleasure that made me blush and shy away.

He was a manly man. He didn't shy away from touching me even in public. Something I didn't quite get accustomed to.

"You haven't answered Ruby. "

"Mm.. " That's what came out when I tried to talk as he ran his hands on the back of my waist and curled them around me before pulling me back.

Right between his legs. I hear the wood break under the blazing fire in the mantle, hinting how quickly time had passed, he felt the warmth fill inside me.

"I fell ill, scarlet fever. But I pulled through. But my mother forbade me from visiting it again."

"I used to cut ice with my uncle at Louis Lake."

I smiled.

"It must be very cold.. "

I refrained from questioning him. Choosing to stick with small comments that would avoid any silence from him.

"Yes. But we adapt young. "

"How far is it? "

"Couple of hours," He said before picking me up and carrying me to bed.

A short gasp escaped my mouth as my back hit the bed. My curls covered my bare chest whole he took my chemise off.

I was still nervous before him. No matter what state. I was always hanging by the edge whenever he was never.

So imagine my state when I was lying bare before him, his hands touching me. Claiming my body as forcefully as he could because I never stopped him. I didn't wish to.

My cries echoed through the chamber as he bit along my thighs to my stomach.

"Please not there-" I beg of him to leave my waist alone. It was too sensitive but he hushed me.

His hand covered my mouth as he bites and sucks on my skin. It hurts but I liked it.

I felt so helpless next to him. I felt weak. My body would give myself up to him without my mind's consent. I seemed to have developed a dual personality for his presence.

Scared, yet getting pleased out of intimidation.

I cried out as he slapped my bum. Before pulling me down and taking me from behind.

"No..." My weak moans were his melody perhaps. Because he would kiss me as I cried out.

"No more...Please? I can't ...Sir" I was begging when he curled her fingers around my neck tight, his eyes turned so scary as he pounded inside me so roughly I felt all of it. Not to mention the occasional bites over my breasts as he took pleasure in it.

"What do we say, Baby?"

That whisper, almost like a groan in my ears made me shiver.

"Please, Sir.."

I was lying on my front, my hair sprawled across my shoulders, my rear covered lightly by the thick woollen blanket. But I wasn't cold. Our action had made the chamber a heating pod. The fire had begun to die, pulling us in a dark warm state. Only the moonlight brightened the end of the chambers.

I felt his hands run against my hair, slowly travelling down my spine, right above the blanket. He pushed it off fondling my bum. I squeeze the pillow under me in my hand. My face dug further down into that soft pillow to hide my content self. He squeezed them, ran his hands through the back of my body unceasingly, like he was studying my body under him. With his head over my back, I felt like a pillow being pampered.

I wanted to remember every bit of it. I was informed the king would be taking up a short travel possibly lasting a week or two in some time. I was dreading those days. For I had not been under any scrutiny as a result of his behaviour towards me. I heard the King had passed a rule to forbade gossip against my Maiden Kingdom or me in general.

I was thankful for it, but it might be futile. People may restrict talk, but one cannot restrict gossip.

His kisses distract me from my pessimism, a smile painted on my lips, my head still dug into that pillow as his lips reached down to my cheeks. He kissed them before an audible wince left my lips as a result of his bite.

I turned my head pushing away his head from my bum but he didn't budge. I cried holding back my laugh at the ticklish feeling of pain while he continued licking and biting right on my bum.

It seemed like I wouldn't be left with just a few marks. He had covered my breasts and stomach. back, now my bum, and also my neck with marks. Not to mention my shoulders. My thighs had multiple.

"That's the twentieth !" I pout eyeing him.

He kissed that aching area before lifting his dark eyes on me.

I gulp at those predatory eyes. Like he would pounce on me like a lion-no, like a wolf. Like he was.

"You should forget the counting my dear" A husky voice entered my ears almost melting my body and mind. I held back my moan while he climbed up my body and turned me around to kiss my neck.

I wince at the fresh bite under my ear. I already kenned how dark and sore that would be.

"No-!" My voice gave up as he pushed open my legs and settled between them. His lips licked me as I shook my head pushing his head away.

"No no..not again-" I knew that was dangerous. Pushing him away.

He grabbed my hand pinning it down on the bed and looked up licking me.

"You stop me again and I'll make your cheeks red and fuck your ass"

Well, that was enough to shut me up. But not enough to stop me from moving under his actions. My legs would close causing him to slap my thigh. I gasped throwing my head back and closing my eyes at the pleasure his mouth gave me. He squelched my jittery body. But he didn't stop.

"It's sore" I whine but he lightly slaps my cheek.

If any man were to do that I would be keening his gems. BUT HIM! Dear lord I was turned into a masochist.

~*~

 # HEAVY SEXUAL CONTENT #18+

"Fuck" His brawny body ever amazed me, I kneeled over the ground, taking his manhood in my mouth, licking it over the tip causing him to fist his fingers in my hair. He sat over the armchair before the newly lit fire, in all his naked glory, as my eyes stared up at him his toned muscular body emphasized before the light.

I found many things about him sexually pleasing, when he flexed his arms pulling them behind his head and leaned back watching me suck him, his veins would pop. When he threw back his head every time I circled his tip with my tongue his Adam's apple would budge.

He would breathe heavily pushing his muscles in and out. Everytime he fists his hand around my hair or neck tight as I took him all in. His gruff voice would groan as I kissed it and let myself get carried away.

"Fuck baby."

I didn't know if I would like to do such a dirty obscene act. Me would was brought up to only bed the King and never expect pleasure or even the thought of enjoying something.

I was wandering a night before through the corridors unable to sleep and needing a book to help me snooze when I saw a young maiden on her knees at the corner of a small chamber. I was aghast, wondering if he was hurting her until Lydia pulled me away.

To say I was bewildered that such a thing was possible would be an understatement.

"Women do that?" That was my question.

She had told me so much that night as we talked till our eyes closed it caused my thoughts astray.

I couldn't stop thinking of it. Perhaps I had become a bit perverted but it is only natural yes? Embarrassed I was as I stared at it twice making me jump back as we sat before the fire after our exhausting act and then cold as the fire had long ceased, I did not want the servants in our quarters this late or simply for the fact that I was a mess and had no intentions of putting on my things to let them in. Watching him toss the log into fire and lit it slowly was fascinating but I digress.

My inner mind laughed at me.

"Do you wanna touch it?"

I was scared to even look, but as I laid there, enjoying the warmth of fire over his chest, my hand did touch it. Simply to feel it.

I saw his eyes closed, his hand tightened around my neck as he sucked in a deep breath. But when I moved my hand up and down as Lydia had suggested, he stopped. I gulp looking at him, ready to apologise, " You have to make it wet before you play with it baby"

"Wet?" I asked

He smirked kissing my lips, squeezing my neck once, "You have to lick it." He commands.

I didn't resist, I couldn't for that fact.

But his eyes shifted, a bridge between his brows as I pushed myself up and got on my knees. He immediately sat up holding my wrists.

"Don't-" He stated.

But I stared up at him, my brows arching up,"Can I please take it in my mouth?"

I genuinely asked, I didn't know how dirty it sounded. But that pleased him. Running his finger through my hair as he sat before me and watched me lick it, taste him and take it in.

I liked watching his lose himself every time I licked across his tip, I saw a side of him I could never imagine. When he would push his brows together and moan cursing his his breath. Or when his hand would grab my hair pushing my mouth further.

I liked it.

"Take it all in like a good girl. All of it"

I gagged pushing away and letting the liquid drip down my chest. I was gasping as it travelled down my stomach.

"Up" He commands grabbing my hair and pulling it, I whined and tried but he turned me pushing me against the way next to the mantle and arching my back.

A loud slap echoes through the chamber. I wasn't much embarrassed. The maids never sleep near us. And the guards cannot hear much due to the heavy walls of the castle.

I cried out in pain as he held my neck from the back and took me right there, Standing.

"No no no-" I could feel it hurt but build up a release in me. As I cried and begged for him to go slow, he never listened.

"Take it all in baby. No excuses"

I gasped shutting close my eyes and whimpering as he pushed in further. It was a mix of pure pleasure and pain. I had my release, something I couldn't explain to myself. I felt wetness pool inside myself. Which wasn't his. This was different.

"Did - did you-" I moaned as he pulled out and I felt it over my ass.

"No, my love-" He kissed my forehead picking me up and carrying me to bed, "I didn't shoot my seeds inside you. I respect your decisions more than anything-"

I frown. "Why did I feel so wet inside-"

He stared at me, laughing and kissing me. "Because I fuck you good enough," He said wiping my bum and pushing the cloth to lightly drag over my soreness and I wince hiding my face.

"It hurts" My muffled voice said.

"Like it fucking should"

It was possibly past midnight as we lay in bed, my body couldn't move, I was far too tired. I was content with sleeping on him, hearing his heartbeat. The sudden loud sound of wolves howling pushed me out of my sleepy state as I opened my eyes sitting up and pulling the sheets closer, scared and looking out the windows, although I couldn't see anything. I knew it was coming from that side of the castle.

My fear raised as I heard loud noises.

Xerxes raised his head and listened before the noise stopped. His arm around my shoulder as I gulp staring at him in worry.

"Sleep. Its nothing"

"But-"

He flipped us over, distracting me from that and kissing my neck.

"the guards have taken care of that."

"What was it?"

"Rouge Wolves attacking the boarders like brainless cunts" He comments chuckling and closing his eyes, his hands busy focusing on my tender breasts.

"why do they revolt against the crown?" I asked

"Some have personal reasons. Some support my enemies."

I see..

I wondered why they turned like that, from human form. But I didn't wanna question much. I hated the thought of over-questioning someone.

"What's bothering you?"

"Nothing" I answer earning a bite for lying right over my buds. I wince covering it and looking at him.

"What is it, my love?" He asked again, challenging me to lie again as he pushed my hand away and kissed my aching bud,

"how does it work? Why are they in the body of a wolf? Like are they human? "

He chuckled Lying beside me and propping his head over his hand. His hand resting over my stomach.

"Our animal form is much stronger, it would be obvious they assume their true form."

"hmm.."I hummed staring at his fingers over my torso.

His hands were so big.

"Our bodies contort."

I never could fathom the fact that they could just turn... into a bloodthirsty predator.

"D-did you-" I stretched my words hesitant t ask a personal question. But his eyes urged me to continue, "Turn like that?"

"I am the Lycan King Ruby, if I couldn't I wouldn't be the king-"

My gut fell. What if his heir couldn't? What if I can birth to a human? Would he then resort to engaging with one of their kind just for the sake of the Kingdom? I do accept it. I always will, Kingdom came before feelings yet, it brought fear into my mind What if that was unaccepted? Me giving birth to a human was unacceptable?

Dread settled in me and I knew he noticed.

He cupped my face kissing my lips softly.

"What if I give birth to a human?" I asked as he froze.

"What if it doesn't work? What if I can't give you an heir?"

"Ruby" His call stopped my thoughts.

"Our baby shall be the next King or Queen of my Throne, Human or not. A king doesn't have to be extraordinary to rule over his kingdom. He just needs to be sharp. Which He or she will be under my eyes"

"Xerxes You do not understand, having a human on the throne of lycan will lead to revolts-"

He chuckled nonchalantly. "The blood of a royal matters more than if the king can turn into a wolf. "

I looked away but he grabbed my jaw facing me towards him.

"This is the least of worries my Queen. I shall get my heir no question."

"but-"

"The rule to have a True Lycan over the thrown was to avoid tainting the blood of the family. You are not the only human this royal family has."

"I-"

"You certainly make me speak a lot my dear, Quite the talent."

I closed my lips shut taking it as a warning.

"Leave your worries up to me. "

When I woke up, I was alone. Before sorrow could settle in me due to the disappointment of not waking up next to him I hear the sounds in around the bed. The curtains of the bed were drawn shut. I frown thinking of I should go out or not. But one side suddenly opens making me jerk back and cover myself. Not that I needed to, The blankets were already over me.

It was him.

He didn't talk, sliding in and closing the curtains before pulling me to lay over him under the sheets.

My body ached terribly. The sore pain between my legs was unbearable. I just needed a hot bath. I sigh closing my eyes as he runs his fingers through my hair.

"Would you like to have breakfast or a bath first?"

He asked them to prepare it for me.

"Bath-" I whispered nothing wanting them to hear it.

He nods. He was wearing a thick robe. His torso is visible and bare, his hair messy. A drowsy look in his eyes.

"P-Perhaps you could sleep a little longer?" I asked softly concerned about him leaving for work after little sleep.

He looked down at me and squeezed my cheeks, "I'm not leaving you today"

My heart melted. I wanted this so bad, ever since our little riding excursion, I was begging the lord to grant me some time with him. Was it so bad to ask for a day to lay around with your husband? A man you possibly were falling in love with.

"No work today Your Majesty?" I asked taking the water in my hands as he pulled me back after getting in behind me.

"No." a curt reply disappointed me. Perhaps he was grumpy in the morn-ing. I use to be as well once.

"An envoy from Your Kingdom shall arrive within the month-" I turned to look at him as he kissed my shoulder, "You shall be the guest to a ball, celebrating the success of our treaty. It will be in your honour. I want you to be alert. Rest I shall have Andrew explain"

I said nothing but nodded.

I bite my lip, blushing before the King as I sat almost naked eating fruits. He had helped me out of the bath and carried me to the couch. When I covered myself with the thin wet fabric he ripped it off me. It landed over my thighs. Covering nothing but my bum and a bit of my lady. Eating naked was nothing but an arousing and embarrassing act.

I could feel his eyes over my body. And when I accidentally dropped some juice from melons he didn't take a second licking it off my breast. I leaned back, on my hands as he assaulted my breasts yet again. Although tender and sore, the pain wasn't enough to shadow the pleasure is mouth gave me.

"I could do this all day"

Dont...I might go crazy.

"They hurt"

"As the fucking should my baby"

I should smile creep in my lips before his harsh bite brushed it off again.

***

"Madam"

Lydia's gentle call woke me up from my deep sleep. I felt tired as if my body was hurting. As I looked at her she smiled waiting for me to sit up and wrap myself in the robe she held. The minute I tried to sit up the pain in my lower belly initiated. I groan holding the sheets to my body as I was naked while she helped me sit up. Pain shout up my stomach making me shut my close and hold my stomach.

"Godness, Your hair is a mess, Madam." She mutters running her hand over my head smoothing my nest out. I chuckled embarrassed.

Of course, it was. From what I recall, I didn't quite get a break last night.

"Oh.." I said looking down and understanding why my condition was that bad.

I look at Lydia in pain and then at the ladies preparing my robes for today,"Ask them to leave-"

"It's alright-"

"No..i-its embarrassing-" I whispered when she realized what I meant.

"You may leave" She stated before rushing them out and coming to my aid.

"It hurts so bad-" I groan standing up and looking back to see blood over the sheets. I was embarrassed to even think about what the king did after he found out. What if he hated me? What if he saw this mess?

"This so embarrassing Lydia. What if His Majesty left early because of this? How am I show my face-"

"The King? Madam, he left just an hour before I woke you up. I do not think he even knows"

I sigh lowering myself in the hot bath and closing my eyes as she tends to my hair.

"I must let the King's mother know about your monthly passes Madam. I was told to do so by her ladies-in-waiting."

I frown looking back, "Why?" She shrugged.

"I suppose they would want to know if you are with child?"

"I do not wish to approve"

"As you wish-"

Ever since my childhood, we women have kept such things away from others' ears. Our Queen from back home kept it from the court until the very date itself. I didn't wish to be a hanging frame for everyone to see in this court. My cycles were nobody's business. I hated the thought of anybody knowing. Or so I wanted... I should say.

I smile at the Dowager as she bows at me slightly, standing in the middle of the ground halls.

"I hope you are in good health." She didn't answer to my greeting.

"And I hope you are with a child soon. Since this month is obviously wasted.." She said looking down at my stomach. My hand immediately presses over my belly while I stare at her in confusion.

"I assure you the court will have their heir -"

I gulp as she steps ahead, I feel my heart beat in my ears as she smirks.

"You, my Queen have no place here without a child in your womb. I have my eyes on you and you better learn to obey our court rules." Her eyes glanced at Lydia once. It irrked me.

"DO not let them take control over you Ruby"

I breathe out and smile again, "There will be no need for that Madam, That particular knowledge shall be privy to me and only my staff, I know my duties very well and I assume you have your own to fulfil. You shall be the first to know if I am with child, you will need no further news apart from this." my curt reply was surely disrespecting to her as she looked at me with such condescending eyes, But all I could do was give her a slight bow in respect and leave.

I was scared for my life while I stood before her, but I had to remind myself of my position. My queen didn't prepare me to be a feeble woman.

As we passed the halls of the east wing and entered the gardens I turned around halting the others behind me in surprise.

"Was that disrespectful? Was it that bad?" I asked Clara as Lydia's feared expression gave away her thoughts.

My eyes flicker from Clara to Fred but he stands nonchalant.

"No Madam. It wasn't." I nodded before turning around and walking to my library.

"Did you tell anyone?" I asked Lydia and she shook her head.

"She wouldn't need to Madam, There are many maids who are loyal to the Dowager. Of course, she has her ways." Clara stated flipping through a book.

These past few months Clara had begun to feel at ease next to me. She wasn't as rigid as before. Finally spoke her mind and gave me her opinion. I was happy since I would rather have an opinionated woman than a quiet one by my side. Especially when it is her.

"You mean to tell me the Dowager might know everything about me including my cycles just because of my maids?"

She nods once.

It filled me with anger, I did not wish to be a daily news to her.

"Fredrick, find me that woman who would love to gossip about her mistress's life more than being a quite loyal woman to her mistress."

He held his laughter back before leaving.

"I must under the orders of My king whom I show my allegiance to, tell you that it is important you conceive. If the King does not want a child It is not simply because he might respect you. It might also be in his personal interests. " Fred leaned down and whispered before leaving.

I sigh nodding. I knew that very well yes. But until I felt ready, I would not be having that conversation with him.

"Madam, it will not be easy. She is the Dowager." Lydia stated.

"Yes, well I am the Queen. And I simply do not wish to be an entertainment to them."

I bite my lip watching him sit in his chair in his study and read something. I hadn't gotten the chance to see the King ever work. He looked charming to me, but I suppose terrifyingly.

The swords of the guards crossed before me as I stepped near the slightly agar door making me flinch and step back.

"Our Apologises My Queen." He stated.

Ah yes, I couldn't enter unless I was asked to. The door suddenly opened wide, revealing Sir Andrew, His eyes went wide before he bowed and waved the guards off.

"Never cross the Queen. She needs no permission Do you need a lesson on the new rules set of you simple ignorant" He grits eyeing the guards menacingly. The guard clearly under his eyes apologises profusely but I laughed to lighten the situation as the guard kneeled suddenly.

"They are doing their duty, No worries. I was only passing back. Now then, take care-" I was about to leave when He stopped me.

"Your Majesty, the King awaits your presence" Andrew stated before opening the door completely for me, revealing Xerxes, staring towards us in scorn.

Well shit.

"You are dismissed" I whispered to Lydia and Clara.

"Good afternoon your Majesty" I greet standing before him and he leaned back on his chair.

"Come here," He said patting his thigh.

I obey without a second thought.

But I wasn't even announced. How did he know?

I quietly sat over his leg and suddenly felt myself blush. He seemed indifferent to what happened in our sheets just some time ago. He leaned back staring at me with a quizzical brow while I hid my eyes in shyness. Not to mention how my maids had seen his marks cover my body while was taking a bath. That was embarrassing.

"How are feeling?" He asked taking my hand

"Well" I replied, I was feeling the worst cramps ever. My stomach hurt. My legs were numb due to my first day. I was on my way to sleep before he invited me in.

"Hmm..then"

I started pushing him back as he hoisted me up on his desk. His face right before me as I panic. He kissed me roughly, pulling down my dress neckline before peppering me with kisses, from my collarbone to my swollen chest.

"No-" I whispered as he pushed my hem up and placed his hand over my thigh. I pulled back holding his hand.

"No, I am not -" I clear my throat.

"I am riding the crimson river today sir"

He froze for a second before pulling his hands back and pulling my hem down with it. Wrapping his hands around my waist and giving it a squeeze.

"Then what are you doing promenading about?"

"I was on my way to my gardens. For some tea"

He nodded.

"You should rest Ruby"

I nodded biting my lip and he fixed my cleavage pulling my dress and kissing me once before helping me down his desk.

"Where did you come from?"

I gulp looking at him. I didn't want him to know I came from the royal court halls. He didn't like me conversing with insignificant people. I suppose it had something to do with my views influencing them and causing misunderstandings.

"From the grounds. I was taking a stroll"

"I do not like you taking a stroll on command grounds Ruby you know that. "

I nodded suddenly trembling under his eyes.

"No more walking on the grounds where my personal guards cannot see you. Yes?"

"Yes"

"Good girl" He said kissing my forehead.

‖CHAPTER 33‖

A few days later]

There I stood before the Princess's library. I breathed out before opening the door and seeing her working while Oliver stood by. She looked up and stood up giving me the usual greetings and I smiled.

I had not been out of my chambers much as I cooped up with delicious food and maids at my disposal at the command of my King. I was very much thankful for it for I had terrible bleeding days. So much so I couldn't move sometimes.

However I had wished to see her Highness very much. As soon as I felt better I was on my heels to her study.

"Your Majesty. You should've called on me" she stated with a frown but I shook my head.

"I was just wondering what you were up to".

In reality, I had received the news of Lord Vincent on the castle grounds again. I thought maybe being with her till he left would help her avoid him.

"Going through the season's report Madam. Would you like to take a look."

I walked next to her and went through the pages however I wasn't looking at them. I was staring at her hands as they flipped the paper.

A new bruise next to her wrist. I frown at it and look at her but she was busy looking at the book before us.

I licked my lips and turned to Fred," When was the last time Lord Vincent paid the court a visit?"

I saw her eyes snap up at me. I could see her body instinctively flinch at the name.

Oliver was the one to speak up, " Two days ago Your Majesty."

He knew what was going on as well.

I nodded looking at the report before smiling at Regina.

"Your Highness, I will be in my private gardens today at noon. Take my mind off work-" I continue as I walk away and towards the door before turning around." I would love to have you. My ladies baked some delicious pastries. I would be happy to share them with you over tea. "

She stayed quiet, with a hesitant expression.

"I..."

"You do not have to decide now. But you are welcome whenever you like. Ionly wish you relaxed, take a day off and enjoyed my garden and some new tea. Surely you can be spared from your other duties to spend time with me."

She smiled but seemed dejected.

"Well. See you then." I bid my farewell and left.

There was nothing more I could say to convince her. But the more I insist the more she would be uncomfortable. It was best I left it up to her.

And if that didn't work. I had other plans.

"Maya, have you asked the cook to-" I turned to see Lydia instead.

"Where is she ?"

" Forgive me Madam she was in the library before we left. Perhaps left to see the cook herself."

I didn't know she was that fast.

Well ...

"You can leave Fred. I wish to walk a bit"

He nodded before leaving us. I would never be comfortable knowing Vincent Clark was on the ground. But I had Clara with me.

I needed Fred to do much more important work than just follow me around.

"Might suggest asking Sir Fredrick to guard her Highness for the time being?" Clara asked as we entered my lounge.

I sit on the couch, grab my book and smirk at her.

Quick witted isn't she?

"I have already asked him to do so." She nodded standing back.

"Madam, the cooks are ready for high tea" Maya walked startling me.

I do not remember asking for her presence. But I suppose it was good since everything was prepared. All I had to do was wait, wait to see if Lord Clark approached her Highness before she came to me.

And I didn't expect that to happen so soon. Hearing the glass doors slam open grabbing my attention, my heart stop as she stood there. Her eyes watering, her face holding sorrow.

I ran to her, grabbing her hand and dragging her towards the private table away from everyone else while Clara followed us.

There was no sign of Fred as he ought to have.

"What happened?" I didn't bother circling around the bush as she sat before me.

"N-nothing. Just, one of those days-"

"I know what happens behind those close doors Regina. And If you don't speak up to me I cannot help you."

She froze pulling away her hand which I was holding lightly, "No your Majesty must have gotten the wrong idea-"

I sigh in disappointment."I shall not ask if that makes you uncomfortable. You may stay here as long as you wish. But I will not sit back and see a man hurt women."

"No! You can't say that-"

"Clark Vincent clearly hurts you-"

"He is to be my husband!"

Everything fell silent as she stood up, turning around to hide her face from me. But she couldn't hide her face from Clara.

I heard her sniff and rub her tears away, "I -I am very grateful for the invite and help, however, It would be best if your Majesty stays away from the internal matters of court. Which I believe are not in your hands."

I frowned but there was nothing I could say.

"I see, surely. There must be many things I do not understand." I whispered earning her attention.

"You do not." She said walking out the door and walking past Fredrick.

I watched her leave before turning to him, "Many here follow his orders. He will be bestowed the title of a Viscount soon. The Dowager made a promise to hand her daughter for protection."

"Protection?"

"If she marries anyone but him, many who support her will not have relevant positions once her husband's family takes over. Queen Dowager wants to make sure the power stays in her family's hands."

"Why these politics when she can ask the King-"

"The king disposed of a highly trusted Viscount just weeks ago under suspicions of producing counterfeit currency. He was very close to the Dowager and hence a supporter of her power in court"

I sigh leaning back in my chair.

"I suppose Her Highness is being used as a pawn to gain back authority," Clara stated.

"I did not know Clark Vincent held such a pristine position."

"Their family has been a part of the primary court decisions for decades Madam. He cannot and will be disposed of just by mere speculations. His family is deeply rooted in the royals"

"Your Majesty, Oliver asks for an audience -"

"Granted" I didn't let the guard finish since I knew what was to be expected of him.

He was after all my spy in this,"Madam-" he bowed.

"Where is she right now?"

"Back in her room your majesty. With Lord Vincent and The Dowager Queen"

He gave us some trivial matters before concluding.

"Thankyou Oliver, you may leave"

He nodded, looking at Fred before leaving.

I huff rolling my eyes, "I suppose I can do nothing and just watch her-getting abused! "

How could this be so complicated? Surely I could help in some way.

Suddenly it dawned on me, I sat up and looked at Lydia. "I am to dine with the King and his cousin today yes?"

She nodded slowly.

"I heard his cousin was the first man to propose to her Highness. Am I right?"

"But, your Majesty might just complicate things if the Dowager learns about your invitation, Knowing what happened. Won't that simply state you support that union"

"Right now Fred, Bringing the King's attention to Regina's wounds is the very best I can do."

"What if Queen Dowager learns of your tactic," Clara asked.

How can she, the only people who know about you all? Lydia would never, Fred is the one who gave me such tactics, Clara and Lady Regina were childhood friends as I just found out a few days ago.

My eyes settled on the doors.

"I suppose no one will" I mutter standing up and walking out to see the guards and my Ladies-in-waiting.

I trusted them but perhaps now, I do not.

"Madam, Your presence is asked in the west wing by Queen Dowager."

I look at the messenger and then at Fred. Nodding before walking out the doors he stopped us.

"She has requested only Her Majesty and Sir Fredrick. You are dismissed as of now."

Clara snaps her head at me before looking back at him, "I cannot be dismissed by anyone but the King"

"You cannot defy the Queen Dowager's commands, you shall have your neck under a sword otherwise."

"You dare-" I stopped her.

"It won't be long. I suppose you know who to go to." I whispered before leaving her.

She stayed quiet as we were escorted towards the far west of the castle.